THE EYEBALL COLLECTOR

Also by F. E. Higgins

The Black Book of Secrets
Winner of a CBI Bisto Book of the Year Honour Award
www.blackbookofsecrets.com

The Bone Magician
www.thebonemagician.com

F. E. HIGGINS

THE EYEBALL COLLECTOR

www.theeyeballcollector.com

MACMILLAN CHILDREN'S BOOKS

First published 2009 by Macmillan Children's Books
a division of Macmillan Publishers Limited
20 New Wharf Road, London N1 9RR
Basingstoke and Oxford
Associated companies throughout the world
www.panmacmillan.com

ISBN 978-0-230-53228-1

1 3 5 7 9 8 6 4 2

A CIP catalogue record for this book is available from
the British Library.

Typeset by Tracey Cunnell
Printed and bound in the UK by CPI Mackays, Chatham ME5 8TD

To Beag Hickory,
Here's to your eyes,
may they never be in your potatoes

Juniper Water or Gin

(*Also known as* Mother's Ruin, kill-grief, comfort, heart's ease, Devil's sweat *and* diddle)

At one stage gin was considered safer to drink than water, the city water often being contaminated with disease. As it became cheaper and cheaper, it was not long before this highly addictive tipple became known as Mother's Ruin. As a result laws were passed that made it more difficult to sell gin openly. There arose the 'gin pipe' as a consequence: a pipe in the wall beside which was a slot. For a payment in the slot, gin would be dispensed into the waiting cup.

from Urbs Umida. A City Beyond Salvation
by K. B. & G. W. Porter-Scott

CONTENTS

PART THE SECOND: THE HAIRY-BACKED FOREST HOG

Extract from *Myths and Folklore, Flora and Fauna of the Ancient Oak Forest*

PART THE THIRD: THE MIDWINTER FEAST 205
Extract from the Menu at Trimalchio's Feast

A Note from F. E. Higgins

Extract from

A letter from Hector Fitzbaudly to Polly

. . . It was my father taught me how to kill a butterfly. To take it in your hand, unsuspecting as it is, and to pinch it underneath with finger and thumb, at the thorax, to stun it. Then to place the body swiftly in the killing jar, tighten the lid and allow the fumes to finish it off painlessly. Father often asked me to net the butterflies, because I was nimble and had a lightness of touch; they were never damaged when I caught them. It is still a source of wonder to me that, from a lowly caterpillar, such a beautiful creature can come into existence.

Then, when I was older, I learned to mount them. We worked in Father's study, in the comforting glow of the fire and beneath the soft light of the gas lamps. I remember how he gathered together, quietly and unhurriedly, the equipment from shelves and drawers and I laid it out neatly on the desk - boards and pins and paper. Next, with a flourish he would present me with the butterfly, a bright yellow Brimstone or perhaps an Orange Tip, and I would begin.

I knew Father was ever watching closely from behind me and I was always keen to show him that he had taught me well. Slowly, so slowly, I would push the long, pointed insect pin through the middle of the butterfly's body, right between the wings - careful not to rub off the tiny scales that gave them their captivating iridescence - and into the mounting board. Next I would position the wings open, exactly how I wanted them, with their patterns matching, before pinning them in place, one at a time, just behind the larger veins. Finally I would place thin pieces of paper over each wing to prevent its curling up while the insect dried. Father wouldn't say anything, just place his hand firmly on my shoulder, and I always knew from the look on his face that he was pleased.

Father gave me a gift shortly before it all happened - a small ebony cocoon to wear on a cord around my neck. I still have it, and every time I touch it I am reminded of those happier days.

But, Polly, that all seems a very long time ago . . .

The description above of the process of butterfly mounting, a common hobby of the age in which this was written, is to be found in one of a number of letters still surviving from a correspondence between a young lad named Hector Fitzbaudly and the girl called Polly (her surname is never given). I found the letters deep in the heart of the Moiraean Mountains, tied together by a leather cord with the ebony cocoon mentioned above hanging from it. I don't think they were all there, and I cannot say if they were ever sent, but I suspect not.

This revealing bundle is just one of many items I have picked up on my travels since last we met in Urbs Umida, that vile city where I uncovered the mystery of the enigmatic Bone Magician and the Silver Apple Killer. I have travelled further abroad since then and my collection of oddities has grown considerably. It now contains:

1 one wooden leg
2 some incomplete handwritten documents, being a young boy's memoirs, and a black leather-bound book of secrets and confessions
3 a beechwood box containing a personal journal and articles from the *Urbs Umida Daily Chronicle*

4 a silver apple
5 the aforementioned letters and ebony cocoon on a leather cord
6 articles from the *Northside Diurnal Journal*
7 one gold-rimmed and diamond-studded cracked false eyeball

The story that follows relies heavily upon this correspondence. And, together with the false eyeball, what a story they tell! As is often the case, I am left with more puzzles than answers.

But let us tarry no longer! Hector's tale awaits . . .

F. E. Higgins

THE EYEBALL COLLECTOR

A Divided City

Ode to Urbs Umida

Urbs Umida, Urbs Umida!
O City, dark and dank.
Would that I could call you sweet,
But by the holy your air 'tis rank!

I took a boat across the Foedus
And looked into the water.
Two fish I saw but dead they were
And swam not as they oughter.

I walked across the cobbled Bridge
Went in the Nimble Finger.
A fight broke out, I ducked a punch
And thought best not to linger.

Urbs Umida, Urbs Umida!
No matter where I roam,
The Foedus's nostril-stinging stench
Will always lure me home.

Beag Hickory

Chapter One

Southbound

'*Tartri flammis!*' cursed Hector as his stomach tightened in a knot and his chest jerked violently with every beat of his heart. He rotated slowly on the spot, panting from the chase. His nose tingled with the stench that filled the air. Already his ears were pricking to the menacing sounds around him: screeches and wails, scraping and dragging, and the ominous unrelenting moaning.

So this is fear, he thought. In a strange way it excited him.

He stood at the centre of Fiveways, an open cobbled space where five dark alleys converged. It was late afternoon but regardless of the time of day it was difficult to see anything

3

clearly in the strange half-light that bathed this part of the City. Hector had crossed the river only twice before, but had never ventured this far. His mistake had been to give chase to the thieving vagabond who had taken his purse. In a matter of seconds the light-fingered boy had led him a merry dance down the unlit, claustrophobic streets and lanes until he was completely lost.

'Wait till I get my hands on him!' muttered Hector. But he knew he wouldn't. The pickpocket was long gone.

Or was he?

A sudden movement to his right caused Hector to turn sharply. He watched with mounting unease a small dark figure slip out of the alley and come silently towards him. He saw another figure, and another. From each alley they came, ten boys in all, creeping closer and closer to surround him. The leader, the tallest, stepped out from the sharp-eyed encircling pack. He lifted his coat slightly and Hector was certain he saw the glint of a blade in his waistband. The boy spoke with the confidence of one who knows he has the upper hand.

'What's your name, Nor'boy?'

'Nor'boy?' queried Hector. He was surprised at how feeble his voice sounded. He clenched his fists and held them to his sides to stop them shaking.

'Yeah, Nor'boy,' repeated the lad. 'You're from the north side, ain't ya?'

'Oh, yes, of course,' he replied. Then, more boldly, 'As for my name, it is Hector, like the Greek hero.'

The leader was unimpressed. 'So, 'Ector, what else can you give us?'

'Give?' The sarcasm was lost on the boys.

'I likes 'is boots,' said one boy.

'And 'is 'at,' said another, and quick as lightning he produced a long stick and hooked Hector's hat, tossing it artfully to land on the leader's head.

'Hey!' Hector cried out, albeit half-heartedly. He was outnumbered, a stranger in hostile territory. If they wanted to let him go, they would. If not? Well, he didn't like to think where he might end up. He had not dealt with such boys before.

'Very well,' he said slowly, but inwardly thinking fast. There must be some way to appease them. 'You have my purse and my hat. You may have my coat and boots if that is your wish, but in return perhaps you could direct me back to the Bridge.'

Hector's accent seemed to amuse his captors and they

sniggered. The leader came unnervingly close to Hector and poked him in the chest.

'I ain't asking your permission, Nor'boy. If I want somefink, I take it.'

He snapped his fingers and instantly the group surged forward, their eyes shining. Like wild animals they closed in. Hector swallowed hard. He could smell them now, they were so close. He could hear their breathing. His mouth was dry as wood chips. He gritted his teeth and held up his fists, preparing to fight.

Then he felt their hands all over him and he was overwhelmed, struggling uselessly against the onslaught. They patted and pulled his coat sleeves and tugged at his cuffs, jerking him near off his feet. Helplessly he allowed the coat to slip off his shoulders and into an assailant's possession. He watched the boy shrugging it on and dancing around, crowing loudly. Someone pulled hard at his bootlaces, unbalancing him, and he landed awkwardly on the ground where he surrendered his boots wordlessly. They took his watch and chain, his silk cravat and finally his gloves.

'Anyfink else?' asked the leader.

'Only my handkerchief,' said Hector sarcastically, getting

back to his feet. He brushed himself down but knew he looked rather foolish. Inadvertently his hand went to his neck, and the sharp-eyed leader pounced. He reached under Hector's shirt and pulled at the concealed leather string. It snapped and he held it up. A small black object dangled from the end.

'Wossat?'

'It's a butterfly cocoon,' said Hector slowly. He suddenly felt very angry. He didn't care about his other possessions, but the cocoon was different. A gift from his father, he couldn't let it go without a fight. Then he smiled. He had an idea.

'I'll challenge you for it.'

The leader raised his eyebrow. The boys looked at each other and readied themselves.

'Not of fists, of wits,' said Hector hastily. 'A riddle. You can all try to answer it, ten of you against one of me. If you answer it correctly, you may have the cocoon; otherwise you must allow me to keep it.'

The boys exchanged grins and winks.

'It's awright wif me,' said the leader. 'Wot's the riddle?'

Hector had the sinking feeling that he was merely delaying the inevitable. Did rascals such as these honour deals? No matter. He had to try. It was just not in his nature to give up easily. He began:

'There was once a kingdom where it was a crime to tell a lie, the punishment being death.'

His ragtag audience laughed at this. Was that good or bad? Hector didn't know. He went on.

'A young man travelled to the kingdom and heard about the crime of lying. "That is nonsense," he declared to the townspeople. "If I tell a lie, I will not be put to death."

'One of the King's guards overheard his boast and asked him, "Did you say you could evade punishment for lying?"

'"No," replied the young man brazenly.

'"That is a lie!" shouted the crowd and he was arrested and thrown into prison.

'The next day he was brought before the King and a jury of twelve.

'"You have been found guilty of lying," said the King. "You may say one last thing before you die, but be warned: if your statement is true, then you will be given a strong sleeping draught and you will die painlessly. But if your statement is a lie, then you will be burned alive and die screaming."

'The young man spoke only one sentence in reply and the King had no choice but to release him.'

The boys were still, listening hard, and Hector felt a brief shiver of something, almost pride. Yes, they held him captive by force, but he too had them gripped, with his words.

'So, what did he say?' asked a small boy at the front. He was sporting Hector's cravat.

'Exactly,' said Hector with a hint of triumph. '*That* is the riddle.'

There was a long pause. 'It's a riddle all right,' shrugged the leader, and suddenly they all ran off, guffawing loudly.

Hector stood alone and motionless in the gloom. It seemed he was right. Such street urchins did not honour deals. But he was free, and at the realization relief flooded his veins. 'Sly devils,' he murmured with more than a little admiration. 'At least I have my life, if not my clothes.'

Nonetheless, he was coatless, hatless and bootless on the wrong side of the City. He had to get back to the Bridge.

But which way to go?

'Well, Hector,' he said ruefully to himself, 'you wanted adventure and that's exactly what you got.'

North of the river in the City of Urbs Umida, like so many others of his ilk, Hector lived a life of ease and sophistication with few cares. Unlike those others, however, he was not satisfied. He wanted something else. South of the river, as he was now, he thought he might have found it. The littered streets were narrower, the roads potholed, the gutters oozed slime. The buildings, sooty and rundown with broken shutters and windows, were packed so tightly together they created a maze of narrow alleys in between. People hurried through the shadowed streets, hugging their secrets to them and often up to no good. And the stink! But how Hector loved it. For all its horrors, at least it made him feel truly alive.

Suddenly, without warning, a hand rested on his shoulder. Hector whipped around to see one of the boys, the small one, standing behind him.

'Now what do you want?' asked Hector in exasperation. 'My breeches too?'

'Nah,' said the boy, and he almost looked offended. 'I want to know the answer. I'll tell yer the way out of here,' he cajoled. 'It's dangerous round these parts for someone likes yerself. You'll get in worser trouble than wiv us.'

Hector smiled. 'Very well,' he said and told him the answer.[*] The boy screwed up his dirty face in puzzlement.

---

[*] If, dear reader, you would know the answer too, then turn to the back of the book, while I proceed with Hector's story here . . .

'I don't get it,' he said, and before Hector could react the boy pressed something into his hand and ran off.

'Wait,' called Hector after him. 'How do I find my way out of here?'

'Just keep left,' came the shouted reply. 'Past Squids Gate Lane and Old Goats Alley, go through the graveyard and that'll take you back to the river.'

Hector opened his hand and there in his palm lay his ebony cocoon. 'Thanks,' he called, but the boy was gone.

Chapter Two

Gulliver Truepin

Gulliver Truepin went to the window, instinctively taking up a position to one side so he couldn't be seen. From up here on the fourth floor he had a fine view across the grimy City to the sluggish river. Without thinking, he placed his hand palm down on the wall but grimaced and removed it immediately. The wall was tacky to the touch and he hardly dared to imagine what substance it was that could be so sticky. Quickly he wiped his pale and slender hand on his handkerchief.

It was some years now since Truepin had been in Urbs Umida. He had not missed the place and he would not have come back were it not for the fact that in his line of business – the business of swindling – Urbs Umida had more than its fair share of potential victims. Not on this side, however; they were too smart for his game, many playing it themselves. No, thought Truepin as he looked north over the River Foedus to the red tiled roofs and the gleaming doors and the wide white pavements, his target was *them* over the river. The rich were easy pickings, surprisingly simple to trick, blinded as they were by their own greed. They deserved whatever they got.

But first he had to find a way to move more easily among them.

Truepin looked in the small fly-spotted mirror on the wall and pulled up his eye patch briefly to reveal his scarred socket and the false eyeball nestled within. The scar, less raised than it used to be and much faded after all these years, wasn't so bad, but the false eyeball was hardly a pleasant sight. It was dull and yellowing, showing signs of age and its poor quality. He wore it to stop his socket from collapsing, but he was appalled enough by it to keep it covered.

'Not for much longer,' muttered Truepin. The day was fast approaching when he could take or leave the patch. He examined his hairline and ran his fingers through his lank locks. He was not entirely sure that they were quite as thick

13

as they had been before. He tutted and reminded himself that this relatively minor problem was a necessary sacrifice for the financial gain.

You see, Truepin's thinning mane was not down to age but to a travelling pedlar's potion. Truepin had bought the potion hoping that it would cure his ongoing stomach trouble, as the label and the pedlar so enthusiastically claimed. Surprisingly enough the sour brown liquid *had* cured his ills, but the side effect had been rapid and substantial hair loss. In a fury Truepin had made strenuous efforts to track down the pedlar and after three days and nights he came upon the unfortunate man at a county fair. There, Truepin sneaked up behind him and began to throttle him, stridently demanding to know the remedy.

'Stop taking the potion and your hair will grow back,' croaked the pedlar.

'Is that it?' asked Truepin.

'Yes,' he gasped. 'You'll see, it will grow back straight away.' Then he lost consciousness.

Truepin immediately saw a wonderfully twisted opportunity for personal gain and true to form he seized it. When the pedlar recovered (two sharp slaps to the face helped) he took him to the nearest ale tent, plied him with drink and wheedled the recipe for the potion out of him. It was as he suspected: mainly water, with the addition of colouring and one extra ingredient which, he deduced, both cured the stomach and caused the hair loss. Truepin bottled up a few gallons of it himself and set off for the nearest small village. By the light of the waxing moon he poured copious quantities of the potion down the village well and waited in the wooded outskirts. Within a matter of days all who had taken water from the well noticed extreme hair loss . . . but suffered no longer from indigestion. To every cloud there is a silver lining! The village was in uproar, having no idea what was causing their misfortune or how to cure it.

It was then that Truepin made his entrance proper. He posed as a travelling apothecary and sold his own cure for baldness (in essence a bottle of flavoured water) with strict instructions to drink only the remedy and milk for ten days. Of course, having not drunk from the well for over a week, everyone's hair was soon growing back and Truepin was hailed as a miracle worker. He was given rooms in the best tavern, fed the finest food the villagers could offer (not so fine, Truepin thought), consulted on – and paid handsomely for – his wise opinions on all matters ranging from mole-catching to bacon-curing.

The trick with conning people was to know when to stop. And this was a maxim by which Truepin lived. After a week or so he bade the grateful villagers farewell and moved on, his purse much the heavier, to another set of victims, and began the whole charade all over again until he had worked his way back to Urbs Umida.

Gulliver Truepin had spent many years now cheating and lying for a living and had a raft of ruses, disguises and pseudonyms in his arsenal. He had perfected the pawnbroker swindle (a little tricky yet ultimately very rewarding), he had made a pretty penny selling 'genuine' pieces of Noah's Ark and had achieved great success with a dancing ferret (until its untimely death). A master of mimicry from an early age, he had long ago discarded his true accent along with his real identity (he was christened Jereome Hogsherd and had begun his life as a lowly peasant). He could switch at will between one mode of speaking and another, allowing him to mingle with the lowest of the low and, as was his preference, the more elevated of society. He had at his disposal the French nuance – he had once played very successfully the part of a Parisian card sharp – and he could drop his aitches with the best of them.

Gulliver Truepin's success in the field of deception,

of which he was very proud, could be measured by the substantial sum of money he had accrued. Unlike others in the same game, he hadn't frittered it away on drink and women and other questionable pursuits. Gulliver Truepin always had one eye (literally) to the future. And the future was now. He was tired of the nomadic lifestyle and ready to enjoy fully the fruits of his dishonest labours. He wanted to settle down, and not in any average sense of the word. His sights were set much higher than that. All his ordinary cons and swindles so far had been merely the springboard to his grandest change of identity yet and the lifestyle of luxury he had always desired and believed he deserved.

But for all this he needed even more money. To this end he had a plan, the first stage of which was to be executed tonight. It was simple, old fashioned – he found this usually proved most effective – and it would take a modicum of daring and deceit. Hardly difficult for a man such as Gulliver Truepin.

It was that old chestnut. Blackmail.

From his lodgings Truepin could also see the Nimble Finger Inn opposite. He had an appointment there in fifteen minutes. He went to the bed, where two sets of clothes were laid out on the coverlet. The quality and finish of each set could not have been more different. On the one side was a smart black velvet jacket and matching breeches, on the other a coarse greying shirt and threadbare waistcoat. He ran his hand over the velvet regretfully. But this was not the time to indulge his taste for quality. He pulled on the latter outfit delicately, as if he could hardly bear the feel of it on his skin. Over these clothes he threw a tatty brown cloak. He looked down at the accompanying boots, worn and scuffed, and shook his head.

'Not long now,' he thought, 'and I can cast off these rags for the last time.' He could endure this discomfort because he knew that the end was in sight.

The light was fading as Gulliver crossed the road. A dark-haired young boy with piercing eyes, oddly underdressed for the weather, bumped into him halfway across. Truepin, suspecting a pickpocket, grabbed him and snarled at him menacingly before releasing him roughly and slipping into the Nimble Finger. He purchased a jug of ale (he would have preferred sparkling wine, of course, but it was not available) and took a seat in a dark corner. His dress ensured that he blended in with the crowd. Easily done too, for no one in the Nimble Finger wished to draw attention to him or herself. Truepin waited, sipping distastefully at his warm ale.

'Truepin?'

He looked up to see a stout fellow in a dark coat and hat swaying over the table. He nodded. The newcomer slid clumsily in beside him.

'Ale?' offered Truepin, though he suspected from the man's drowsy demeanour and reddened nose that he was already gin-sozzled enough.

'Aye,' came the gruff reply. Truepin poured another cup.

'So,' said the man after a long noisy swig, 'I believe you want a new name.'

'I do.'

'And a title?'

'Indeed.'

'It'll cost yer, and cost good,' the man slurred.

Truepin nodded. 'I have the money.' Or I will soon, he thought.

'Then it is done. Come back at midnight – it'll be ready.' With that the fellow swallowed the other half of his ale and disappeared into the crowd.

Truepin sat back and allowed himself a moment to smile. And so it begins, he thought. Now for the next stage. A change of clothes and off to the dwelling of Mr Augustus Fitzbaudly.

Chapter Three

Northside

Hector sat motionless in the butterfly house. He was hot, almost uncomfortably so, despite being in his nightshirt. His feet were sore, cut to shreds from his barefoot run home, and his nerves were still on edge. All around him flew butterflies of every size and hue alighting on the luscious plants and flowers that grew up the glass walls of their home.

Such beauty, thought Hector, and yet only a short while ago he had been surrounded by ugliness and enjoying that too . . .

The journey home from the south had felt interminable. Loping along, head down, trying to avoid looking anyone in the eye, Hector had still attracted plenty of unwanted attention. Not because he had lost his clothes, but because those that were left were so clean. There were plenty of badly dressed boys about, but none with such white stockings. But soon enough, on account of the piles of manure and rotten vegetables on both street and pavement, he looked no different to the numerous other guttersnipes ducking and diving in and out of the crowds. Hector had just learned, like everyone else, that in this place it was often better not to stand out.

He passed riotous taverns and unlit shops and pawn-brokers' windows. He looked down alleys and saw crouched and still figures, dead or alive he couldn't tell, and strange shadows at the gin pipes gulping down the fiery liquid that warmed the throat and dulled sorrows before inevitably leading to their downfall. He dodged carts, milkmaids, foul-mouthed beggars, knife-grinders and travelling players.

When he finally reached the river Hector allowed himself to think for the first time that he might get home safely. He leaned over the low parapet to see up close the dark waters of the infamous Foedus. The smell of the river that day would stay with him all his life. In later years the aroma of just one atom of its chemical make-up would instantly transport him back to Urbs Umida and dredge up bittersweet memories of the south side. For some cities the river was its lifeblood; for Urbs Umida it was more like the Styx in the Underworld and Hector's fervent imagination momentarily conjured up Charon, the mythological ferryman of souls, and his punt poling down the river. When he looked again he realized it was only a poor river-taxi man.

Halfway across the bridge, as he passed under the sign of the Nimble Finger Inn, a tavern of such ill repute it was known to all, north and south, Hector knew the end was in sight and it spurred him on. In his haste he tripped on an upturned cobble and lurched into a dirty-looking fellow crossing the street.

'Trying to pick my pocket?' snarled the man, grabbing Hector's arm and pinching his chin to tip his face towards his own. It was not a pretty sight. The man wore a filthy black eyepatch and a grey beard, and he gave Hector a violent shake before releasing him. Hector stumbled off as quickly as his tired legs could carry him until he reached the broad, bright streets of the north . . .

Now, some hours later, safe in his father's butterfly house, the south again was a distant world. Outside the gentle moon glowed through the glass. A butterfly, as black as night, alighted on Hector's palm where it sat quietly. He could feel its legs delicately pinching his skin. It must be newly hatched he decided, and carefully brought it closer to his face for a better look.

'Hector?'

The sound of the voice caused Hector to jump. He looked up to see his father standing in the doorway. The butterfly flew off, ascending in a gentle spiral to the glass roof.

'What are you doing down here at this time of night?' his father asked, a concerned look on his face.

Hector shrugged. 'I couldn't sleep.' Similarly he wondered why his father was out here so late. Hector had noticed that he seemed preoccupied with something these last few days. Business, I suppose, he thought. To divert attention away from himself he pointed to the black butterfly, now settled on the white flowers of a nearby shrub.

'I see you have a new one. *Pulvis funestus*, if I'm not mistaken.'

His father smiled. 'Yes, you are correct. Though it's usually just called Blackwing. Quite striking in large numbers. When they flock together they create a cloud of black dust that has been superstitiously described as like a cloud of death. As you see, they are very fond of *Lippia citriodora*, or lemon verbena as it is better known. They adore its citrusy smell. But it's late. Come back up to the study. I have something to show you.'

The grass was wet with night dew and Hector took off his slippers and walked barefoot to soothe his feet. If his father noticed, he said nothing.

In Augustus Fitzbaudly's study glass cases lined every wall, each case holding a butterfly: dark brown Hairstreaks, ragged-winged Fritillaries, elegant Swallowtails and Painted Ladies. Hector prided himself on knowing all their common and Latin names. Augustus's fascination with lepidoptery, the study of butterflies and moths, started after Hector's mother died. As his father spent more and more time on his collection, Hector realized that to have his attention he too would have to develop an interest in these insects. At first he had been squeamish about some of the practices, but by now he anticipated eagerly the brown-paper wrapped packages stamped in large black letters '*Urbs Umida Lepidopterist Supplies*' containing cocoons, butterfly eggs or caterpillars.

'Here it is,' said Augustus, and he held out a glass case

twice the size of all the others. Within, its huge wings spread in the still symmetry of death, was the largest butterfly Hector had ever seen, its colours a myriad vibrant blues and greens and sparking purple.

'*Papilio ingenspennatus*,' said Augustus. 'Its wingspan can measure up to a foot. Like the Blackwing, it is capable of surviving in the cocoon in very low temperatures, developing fully but not emerging until it is warm enough.'

Hector looked on in awe. He had never seen anything like it. Even in such still repose it seemed to shimmer.

'Did you go over the Bridge today?' asked his father suddenly, catching him off guard. 'I saw you come in earlier. You looked a little dishevelled to say the least.'

There was no point denying it. Besides, was that a twinkle in his father's eye? 'I wanted to see what it was like on the other side, that's all,' said Hector lightly, still staring at the butterfly before him.

'An adventure then. And what did you think? Ugly, filthy, smelly?' Augustus was watching him keenly.

Hector knew that was the answer his father expected. And it was true. How could he forget the ugliness, the grime and the stench? But the very thought sent a thrill of excitement through him too. 'Over here everyone is so polite,' he explained. 'Or at least they pretend to be. The ladies twirl their parasols and show off their new gowns. The men bow and smile and make boring conversation. But it's all a show. They don't mean a word of it.'

'There is probably some truth in that,' murmured his father.

'But over the river,' Hector enthused, 'it's not just that the people look different, it's how the place feels: alive, sort of scary but exciting too. Sometimes life seems half dead this side of the Foedus.'

Now Augustus looked alarmed. He lowered his voice and spoke sternly.

'Hector, don't be drawn in by it. It might feel alluring, exciting, different, but it is vile, *vile*. Every vice known to man is come alive on those streets. The place is rotten to the core, peopled with bibacious gin-swilling wretches and reprobates. In fact, I forbid you to go there again.'

Hector felt his face fall and his father immediately softened. 'Your future is this side, son. I have a place for you in the business.'

'As a wine merchant?' said Hector ruefully. 'But I don't want . . .'

Augustus placed a hand on his shoulder and smiled.

'Don't forget, the wine business has served us well. It provides all we have. If you do not take over the business, then who will?'

The long silence between the two, each disappointed in his own way, was broken by the chimes of the study clock. Hector considered his father for a moment more and, doubting his escapades over the river were the only cause of his father's anger and anxiety, he changed the subject entirely.

'Have you a riddle for me before I go to bed?' he asked. It was a game they played nightly. 'It is your turn.'

Augustus relaxed his furrowed brow. 'I have indeed, and it is a hard one. E.'

'E?' queried Hector with a frown.

'E, plain and simple,' repeated Augustus. 'Can you solve it?'

'Hmm,' mused Hector. 'A single letter. Maybe it has lost its fellow letters.' His father's expression told Hector he was on the right track. 'So how could this be?' he continued. 'Perhaps it comes from a word that has shrunk and all that is left is "e".'

His father grimaced and Hector grinned broadly before declaring, 'I think that word could be . . . *Senselessness*!'

Augustus clapped and laughed. 'Hector,' he said, 'you are without doubt exceedingly clever. I know you have a great future ahead of you.'

'But must I really be a wine merchant?'

'No more buts.' Augustus wagged his finger playfully. 'Off to bed with you. I have a meeting.'

Hector raised his eyebrows. 'This late?'

'Sometimes it has to be done,' his father replied vaguely. 'Come along. I'll see you to the stairs.'

Chapter Four

An Unwelcome Visitor

Upstairs on the half-landing Hector knelt and watched his father return to the study. He had an excellent view of what was going on below but, having turned down the gas light, was himself quite impossible to see. Intrigued by his father's late-night visitor he was determined to catch sight of him. Surely his father's odd mood had something to do with this meeting.

He heard the rap of the front-door knocker and observed, with the keen eyes of youth, the maid usher a man swathed in black along the hall to the study. You could tell a lot about a person by the manner in which he dressed, but Hector found it surprisingly difficult to glean much from the fellow below. His attire was remarkably anonymous. The clothes fitted well but were dark as night. It was as if they sucked in every ray of light that hit them. His wide-brimmed hat was pulled low over his forehead and he kept his head down.

'Hmmm,' mused Hector. 'How odd.' Hector was quite the expert on the apparel of the well-off, the well-off being the only sort of people invited into the house. But this fellow was giving nothing away and it made Hector immediately suspicious. It was not normal for someone to come here without wishing to show off their wealth.

The maid knocked on the study door.

'Mr Truepin to see you,' she called.

The door opened and the shadowy man went in. Hector waited until the maid disappeared and crept down the stairs. He knelt at the study door, put his face against the escutcheon and peered in through the keyhole. He sniffed and picked up the faintest whiff of citrus. He wears perfume, thought Hector, but it was not much to go on.

He could see his father's wide leather-topped desk and his chair but the rest of the room was out of his field of vision. Truepin was on the left, standing sideways to the desk. He had removed his hat and Hector took the opportunity to scrutinize his profile. He noticed the narrow, slightly hooked nose and the jutting-out chin. And then to his surprise he saw that the fellow wore an eye-patch over his left eye.

'What a coincidence,' he breathed. For surely this was the very same man who had glared at him on the Bridge. Better dressed, yes, his beard neatly trimmed, but he recognized the nose. How does a man lose an eye? he wondered. In battle? In a duel for a fair maiden? The truth was far less noble but Hector was not to know that.

He looked at his father, who was standing behind the desk. He seemed nervous, plucking at his lapels, and held a sheet of paper in one hand.

'So you are Gulliver Truepin,' said Augustus coldly.

'I see you received my letter,' replied the visitor.

Augustus's face darkened. 'I did,' he said, 'and such a piece of treachery I never did read before. I have a mind to call the magistrate right now – he is my friend, you know – and have you clapped in irons. Blackmail is the most despicable crime.'

Truepin looked puzzled. 'Blackmail?' he repeated. 'I am surprised at you, Mr Fitzbadly——'

'It's pronounced Fitz-*boe*-dly,' corrected Hector's father through gritted teeth.

'As you wish.' Truepin smiled thinly. 'Perhaps some

would call it blackmail, but I like to think of it as a business negotiation. It is the truth after all, is it not?'

'I do not deal with blackguards,' spat Augustus.

'Then I will have no choice but to take my story to the *Diurnal Journal*,' replied Truepin coolly. 'They will pay for it, I can assure you. I think they would find it most interesting to know that you, Augustus, the northside's favourite wine merchant, the man who supplies every table, every restaurant this side of the river with fine wines and ports, are nothing better than a southside cheap gin hawker!'

Hector watched in horror as his father turned puce in the face of Truepin's dreadful accusation. What was this man talking about? Father a gin seller? It couldn't be! Now Augustus looked as if he might suffer an apoplectic fit.

Truepin continued. 'I know for a fact, Mr Fitz*badly*, that you made your fortune selling gin to the southside masses, encouraging their addiction and profiting from their misery. You own more gin pipes than any other merchant.'

'How do you know this?' spluttered Augustus.

'I have evidence,' replied Truepin, 'and plenty of people to verify my claims. What sort of man would make his money from such a business?'

'And what sort of man are you,' challenged Augustus,

'wishing to profit from threats and accusations? And these people, these witnesses to my transgressions, where are they? All in your pay, I warrant. Perhaps my early wealth was made in this way. I'll not deny I have sold gin in the past, but I was young; I made a mistake. I have tried to make up for it.'

'Ah yes,' sneered Truepin. 'Your donations to orphanages and soup kitchens. Heartwarming, I'm sure. In fact, that is what led me to you. A man of your stature does not pay money to soup kitchens without good reason. Perhaps you are unique in that you have a conscience. But the fact remains, I can ruin you. We all know the fickle nature of the northsiders: friends one minute, enemies the next. But you would be lost without them. Pay me what I ask, or suffer the consequences. Consider it another donation to charity if you like – what I ask must be a drop in the ocean of your vast wealth.'

Outside the door Hector listened to this exchange with clenched fists and gritted teeth. He could hardly believe what he was hearing. Hadn't he seen the gin-soaked wretches today? Could his father really have been involved in such a thing? He had admitted to it, but if he said he regretted it, that he no longer dealt in such things, Hector believed him. As for the amount Truepin demanded, it was substantial, drop in the ocean or not. 'Don't pay,' he urged silently. 'Don't pay such a villain.'

His father paced behind the desk in an agony of indecision. Truepin looked on, his face immobile. Finally Augustus turned and Hector's heart sank when he saw his expression. He could tell immediately what he was going to do.

'Very well, you vile man,' said Augustus slowly. 'I will pay you. But only for the sake of my son and his future. And I'll double what you ask for, on the understanding that you leave the City and never return.'

'Treble it and it's a deal.'

Augustus closed his eyes and nodded. 'I will give it to you but I curse you for the rest of your days.'

Truepin allowed himself a short smile. 'Curse me if you wish – words cannot harm me. Just hand over the money.'

'No!' whispered Hector, far louder than he intended.

Truepin turned. 'Is someone outside?'

Augustus opened the door but Hector was already gone.

Chapter Five

Article from

The Northside Diurnal Journal

A quality daily newspaper for the discerning reader

Not Such a Good Fit
By
Tarquin Faulkner

Over the years the name 'Fitzbaudly' and the words
'Fine Wines, Ports and Vintage Rarities' have become
interchangeable. The good people north of the River
Foedus know that one does not come without the other.
Fitzbaudly is a name to be trusted, to be relied upon, and
a Fitzbaudly wine is guaranteed to be exactly as it states on
the bottle – robust, honest and of superior quality.

Alas, no more the case.

Augustus Fitzbaudly, unlike his wines, is not what he claims to be. It has come to my attention by way of a concerned citizen that despite his airs and graces Augustus Fitzbaudly is a fraud. His money, surely a considerable fortune by now, comes not only from the sale of reputable wines, but from the gallons of cheap, adulterated gin that he sells from his numerous gin shops south of the river. We in the northside are acutely aware of how utterly ruinous is the gin habit, and how it leads one and all down the path to self-destruction. Who amongst us has not seen the drunken, wretched tramps half dead in the street over the river? We have counted ourselves fortunate that they choose to stay with others of their ilk across the water, and we have despaired as to their dreadful situation. But now you know where to lay the blame. Squarely at the feet of Augustus Fitzbaudly.

I call upon you, each and every one, to withdraw your support for Fitzbaudly's Fine Wines. No more should you order his Merlots and his Mataros, his Lambruscos and his Chardonnays, his Yellow Monks or his Black Turrets. It is the very least we can do to help those less fortunate than ourselves. The man is no longer deserving of our patronage.

We have been cheated and it is only natural that we should feel outraged. And there are certainly other reputable wine merchants from whom to purchase your requirements. I can wholeheartedly recommend Faulkner's of Vine Street (no relation).

Chapter Six

A Letter to Polly

Dear Polly,

I didn't tell you much about me during those early days at Fitch's Home, but you suspected all was not as it seemed. As the weeks passed you proved to be a good friend. You listened when I wanted to talk and asked no questions when I didn't. So now I will repay your friendship with the truth – and tell you exactly what happened to land me on the home's doorstep.

It was the day Gulliver Truepin came into our lives that changed everything. I remember vividly the night he visited my father with his threats. Father came up to see me afterwards. He stood in the bedroom doorway looking as if he had aged years in a matter of hours.

'Is everything going to be all right?' I asked.

He sat on the bed and looked at me directly. Perhaps he guessed I had overheard.

'Hector, sometimes a person has to do things that are distasteful. It is part of life's journey. I have regrets about my past but I thought I had put it behind me. The man who came tonight, Gulliver Truepin, is a parasite. He feeds off others' misfortune. But what's done is done. My concern now is only for you. My duty is to see that my errors do not stand in the way of your success and happiness. What I have built I have built for you.'

'I understand,' I said.

But things had changed forever.

So much for honour among thieves. Truepin, having blackmailed my father and taken his money, still sold his story to the 'Diurnal Journal'. I bet they paid him well, for even the merest whiff of scandal is well rewarded in Urbs Umida. Within days every news-sheet in the City carried the story of Father's cheap-gin exploits and subsequent downfall. And although Father was the victim of a blackmailing swindler, he was portrayed as the only villain.

It was precipitous. Like a snowball rolling down a mountain my father's downfall gathered speed and size. No one wanted to be associated with a failure. Orders were cancelled, debts were called in and we were abandoned to our fate. What hypocrisy! But that is what the north side is like. It matters only how you look, not what is underneath, and it is vital never to let your secrets be found out. Father fell into despair and refused to leave the study. The servants abandoned us, like rats leaving a ship. Many were engaged by the neighbours. Mrs Ecclestope claimed our cook — she had always coveted her stuffed goose. Even my tutor disappeared and my days were my own.

Eventually we had nothing left and the sale of our home and its contents was placed in the hands of the solicitors and debt-collectors Messrs Badlesmire and Leavelund. Like vultures descending on a carcass they arrived and all that horrible day I watched every single one of our possessions being removed. Father remained tight-lipped and stoical throughout until they came into his study and began to take his butterfly collection.

'Now, then, Mr Fitzbaudly,' I heard Badlesmire warn. 'No need for a scene, my good man. No need at all.'

But before I could react Father had lunged at him to wrest a glass display case from his arms. As I tried to pull my father back, the case dropped and shattered. The colourful wings of the huge butterfly within, the one Father had shown me so happily only days before, tore against the sharp glass pieces and scattered, staining the carpet with their dust.

Later that night when the house was empty and the invaders had gone, I found Father in the stripped butterfly house, staring into space.

'It's Truepin that's done this,' I told him with venom. 'We must find him and take him to the courts for his lies and blackmailing ways. We must have justice!'

'He will be well gone from this city,' said my father. 'He got what he wanted.' He turned around and I was shocked by his pallor, as if all life was draining from him.

'Maybe the newspapers are right,' he said quietly. 'Maybe I do deserve this.'

'No one deserves this,' I said hotly. 'And who is

41

Gulliver Truepin to sit in judgement on you anyway?' I clenched my fist. 'I swear if I ever find him . . .'

Father shook his head. 'No, violence is not the answer.' He put out his hand and leaned on the wall as if to steady himself. 'To refrain from imitation is the best revenge.'

'What are you talking about?' I was almost shouting but couldn't help myself. 'Surely you don't believe that Truepin should go unpunished?'

Suddenly Father moaned and clutched at his chest, then collapsed on to the stone floor. Instantly I dropped to my knees and took my father's head in my lap. His eyes were wide and staring, his body was rigid and his breathing was harsh and irregular.

'Hector,' he gasped, 'I always feared one day my secret would be discovered. I just didn't realize how bad it would be. I'm so sorry - it was wrong of me.'

I held back tears as I shook my head and told him it didn't matter. His skin had taken on a green hue by now and his lips were blue. He struggled to take my arm, drawing me even closer to hear what he had to say.

'It's too late for me, but it's not too late for you,' he whispered. 'Take heed. I know you're angry now, but remember: when you run with wolves you become a wolf. Is that what you want?'

'I only want justice,' I sobbed.

Father smiled up at me. 'I know you will do the right thing,' he breathed. Then his face contorted in a grimace. His grip tightened spasmodically on my arm. He emitted a long deep sigh, his fingers loosened and I knew he was dead.

In the tenebrous shadows of the butterfly house I gripped the black cocoon at my neck until my knuckles went white. 'Not justice then,' I whispered, 'but revenge.'

Salve,

Your friend,

Hector

Chapter Seven

~ ~

Fitch's Home for Exposed Babies and Abandoned Boys

There were no mourners at Augustus Fitzbaudly's burial
other than Hector. The vicar, grimacing in the rain, read a
short passage from the Bible and hurried away to the shelter
of the church, his performance directly proportional to the
paltry sum he had been paid. In the absence of any other
help, the gravedigger struggled to push the coffin into
the grave, all the time muttering under his breath, until
eventually Hector stepped forward dazedly to help. The
cheap wooden box, already splitting at the joins, sat just
below the grave's edges, no more than three feet under.
Hector not having the money to pay for a single plot, his
father had been buried on top of someone else. He walked

away to the sound of soil landing on the coffin lid. He was deeply ashamed that his father was buried in a pauper's grave and vowed to right that as soon as he had the chance, if he had to dig him up and move him himself.

Hector did not know where he was going and for the moment he didn't care. On he went past the gin shops and the gin pipes, always wondering if they had ever been his father's. He passed beneath ominous street names: Fetter's Gate, Melancholy Lane, Old Goat's Alley, names that were soon to become all too familiar. And in the crepuscular shadows he could see movement and bustle. But he did not feel excitement nor did he feel alive, only half dead and afraid.

Earlier that day he had left for the last time the wide, well-lit streets and the tended squares of the north. He had passed the lines of shining carriages waiting outside the theatres and restaurants (where once Fitzbaudly wines had been served nightly) to cross the Bridge once again.

And now, with his father dead and buried, he felt only disbelief and numbness.

Unhesitatingly he walked on through the misty rain. He heard not one of the cries for help from the wretches all around. He felt none of the grasping fingers that pulled at

45

his coat. Even when a wild-eyed tramp stepped right in front of him, arms akimbo, he paid no heed. The tramp, seeing the desperate stare on his face, dropped his hands and let him be. Eventually Hector sank down on the steps of yet another soot-blackened and dilapidated building and put his head in his hands. He was exhausted. So lost was he in his thoughts that he did not hear the door open behind him. But he did feel the bony arms that wrapped themselves around him and quite literally dragged him inside. The door shut with a resounding bang and the gloom enveloped him.

'Ah, has the good Lord Himself sent us another one?' The cracked voice came from close to his head. 'Don't worry, dearie, we'll look after yer here. Has yer been left out in the cold?'

Hector managed to extricate himself from the woman's surprisingly strong grip (he thought it was a woman – from her voice he couldn't be sure) and turned to take a look at his captor. He realized afterwards when he saw her in daylight that this gloom was in fact the kindest light in which to view her, but for now he could see enough only to make out a short, wizened little figure of the female persuasion.

'I'm Mrs Fitch,' she said. 'I knows what it's like to be on the mean streets of Urbs Umida. I knows yer pain. But the Lord –' here she quickly crossed herself – 'He saved me from meself by the curious means of a tragic accident. I nearly committed a terrible crime but He showed me the way and allowed me to redeem meself. Don't fink it has been easy, oh no, I am tested all the time. And up there –' she glanced heavenward, though in fact her sights were somewhat lower – 'is the greatest trial of 'em all. Poor Ned Upstairs, saved from one tragedy, gone straight into another. Stuck in a useless body.'

'Where am I?' asked Hector when Mrs Fitch stopped talking to take a rattling breath.

'Why, you're in the best place you could possibly be: Lottie Fitch's home for Exposed Babies and Abandoned Boys.'

'But I have not been abandoned,' protested Hector. 'My father has . . . died.'

'Ah, such a tragedy for one so young,' said Lottie, and she gave him another squeeze. 'But don't yer worry, we'll look after yer. Follow me.'

Hector allowed Mrs Fitch to take him along the corridor. He followed her down the stairs into a large kitchen furnished with a long table and benches. All the while she continued to talk about the Lord and her good deeds with an occasional reference to 'Poor Ned Upstairs'.

A girl was chopping vegetables at the far end of the table. She looked up at the sound of footsteps and smiled.

'Ah, Polly,' said Mrs Fitch. 'We have a newcomer. Hector. He needs somefink to eat and then perhaps you could find him a bed. But first let's say a very quick prayer of fanks that he came to us and didn't succumb to the evil streets of the City.'

Instantly Polly stopped chopping and put her hands together and closed her eyes, as did Mrs Fitch, and they both mumbled a quick prayer to the Almighty. Hector, although not strictly a religious child, knew enough to join his own hands and mumble along. Mrs Fitch seemed pleased. She handed him over to Polly and left.

Many abandoned boys had come and gone in the few years since Polly began work at the Home, and she had cared for them all equally, but this boy struck her immediately as different. His dark hair flopped over his face and the eyes that stared out from under the wet fringe were black as coal. Despite his bedraggled appearance he stood erect and looked around with an air of confident enquiry. He was not plump, but obviously well fed; and he was tall, nearly as tall as she was, despite the difference in age, which she judged to be five or six years. In a practised glance she noted that his cuffs reached his wrists (not a child here had a shirt that fitted any longer) and that his cloak was of a high quality and, despite the mud, she could tell that his boots had been recently polished. This Hector, she decided, had lived well until now. He could not have been more different from the other boys at the Home if he had tried.

'Welcome to Lottie Fitch's,' Polly said kindly. 'Would you like something to eat?'

'Yes, please,' replied Hector, realizing that despite his grief he was actually very hungry. He had hardly eaten since his father's sudden death.

Polly brought over a plate of bread and ham and a big mug of milk and set it down in front of him. She continued to chop vegetables and tend to the fire while he ate and drank, but she was watching him. 'You are not from the south, are you?' she said eventually. It was more a statement than a question.

Hector shook his head. 'No. And you sound as if you are from outside the City entirely.'

Polly nodded. 'I come from a village in the Moiraean Mountains called Pagus Parvus. I came to Urbs Umida to find work but it was not as easy as I imagined. I was fortunate to meet Mrs Fitch.'

That makes two of us, thought Hector as he finished his bread. 'Have you a napkin?' he asked.

Polly laughed. 'Use your sleeve. That's what we do. Saves the laundry.' With the side of the knife she pushed all the vegetables into a pot and wiped her hands on her apron. 'Let's find you a bed,' she said. 'You look worn out.'

Polly took a candle for herself and one for Hector and led him up the stairs. It was dark and in her shadow difficult to see.

'No gas lights?' he asked.

Polly shook her head. 'You might find things different here,' she remarked as they reached the landing. 'Don't mind the noises from up there.' She glanced in the direction of the attic. 'It's only Ned.'

'You mean "Poor Ned Upstairs"?'

'Yes, Mrs Fitch's husband. He's in the attic. He fell in the Foedus some years ago, in the middle of winter. They dragged him out but he never fully recovered. He was poisoned by the water and is now abed day and night. Mrs Fitch says that it is his punishment for their sins.'

'What sins?'

Polly shrugged. 'I think it is to do with her son, Ludlow. No one has seen him for years. Oddly enough, he lived in

Pagus Parvus himself for a while when I was there. I suspect the Fitches treated him cruelly, but he never did tell me why he left Urbs Umida. Now Mrs Fitch has visions telling her that she must save the children. Every day nearly. Messages from Above, she says, guiding her.'

Polly lifted the latch on a small door to her right. It was only just as high as Hector. She would have to bend to enter, he thought.

'The other rooms are full at the moment,' she said almost apologetically. 'Three to a bed. You'll probably be more comfortable in here for the time being.'

Hector stepped into the darkness holding his candle before him. In the light of the flame he saw that the room was little more than a space under the stairs.

'By Jove!' he exclaimed before he could help himself (a favourite classical expression of his tutor). 'It's small.'

Polly raised her eyebrow sympathetically. 'But it's warm.'

Hector attempted a smile. Whatever the size, it had to be better than three in a bed. 'Thank you,' he said quietly.

'I'm sure you'll get used to it.'

I hope not to be here long enough to get used to it, he thought. Suddenly he felt an indescribably painful yearning for his own bedroom and for his father.

'There's a bell for breakfast,' continued Polly helpfully. 'Afterwards you do your chores and then you must go out and try to earn money.'

'For Mrs Fitch?' asked Hector.

She winked. 'Mrs Fitch takes some, of course. But she can only take what she knows about.'

Hector laughed. Polly looked thoughtful. 'You know, Hector, the boys here – well, they're good-hearted really but they're all southsiders. You, being from the north side – well, you might find that—'

'You think they might take against me because of where I come from?' he finished.

'Well . . . yes. At first anyway.' She went to the top of the stairs and rested her hand on the banister. 'But somehow –' she grinned – 'I think you will survive.' And then she descended into the darkness.

Hector set the candle down beside the mattress on the floor and pulled the door shut. He stretched out his arms and found he could touch both the wall and door in one go. The bricks were warm to the touch. But of course, he thought, the chimney must be on the other side and Mrs Fitch probably has the fire going all day in the kitchen below.

He placed his bag on the floor beside him and lay back on the mattress. He yawned widely and felt the cocoon at his neck. It brought him some comfort these days. Then, as every night now since all his troubles began, he thought of Gulliver Truepin. He doubted very much that *he* was asleep under some stairs.

'Just wait until I find you, Truepin,' vowed Hector again. 'And you will pay for what you have done.'

Chapter Eight

 ━ ━

Metamorphosis

Hector was right. At the same time as he was settling down
in a cupboard under the stairs, in a smart lodging house on
the north side of the Foedus his one-eyed foe was observing
himself in the mirror of a much larger room. Once again,
spread out on the bed coverlet – in this establishment
made only of silk – was an array of clothing, but this time
it had been delivered that day from the City's best tailors
and outfitters. Waistcoats and breeches, shirts and collars
and cuffs, stockings and handkerchiefs – everything a
gentleman's wardrobe should contain. There was much
velvet just begging to be stroked (which he did), soft satins
and silks, felt and linen, all hand-stitched. And what splendid

hues — scarlet and magenta, indigo and mauve, purple and gold and a particularly lovely peridot green.

Having spent at least two quarter-strokes of the clock feeling the clothing, Hector's enemy dressed in blue with scarlet accessories. But the final touch was a coordinating glass eye. He examined again the startling new eyeball that stared back at him in the mirror. It was bright, a perfect fit, and upon closer inspection the twinkle in the pupil proved to be emanating from a small scarlet ruby. This glass eye, an early purchase with his new wealth, was an indulgence, he knew, but what was the use of all his hard work if he could not indulge himself a little? And this was merely the first. Ultimately, he had in mind a collection, one for every day of the week and every outfit. Until he could manage that, he could always make do with his hand-tailored eyepatches between times.

'Good evening to you, sir,' he said to the man in the full-length glass (it was himself, of course), and gave a gracious bow. Then he stood upright and eyed his reflection critically whilst smoothing down the velvet on his thighs and adjusting his frilly collar. He continued his performance, kissing the air where in his mind he judged the gloved hand of a curtsying lady might be.

Curtsying? Before him? Why, yes. You see this fellow play-acting before the mirror was no longer the swindling blackmailer Gulliver Truepin (though there would always be a resemblance, namely the prominent nose). Nay! Gulliver Truepin had been discarded along with his rags and here in his place stood a nobleman of great lineage.

The metamorphosis was complete.

It had been a busy seven days for Hector's enemy. Directly after taking Fitzbaudly's money (trebled, he could hardly believe it!) he had gone back to the Nimble Finger where he received, in exchange for a large chunk of that money, a thick bundle of yellowing lineage papers and documentation. Upon examination of said papers he was delighted to see that they were all written faultlessly in the legal style of the day, with flowery lettering in red and black ink and tied with authentic pale pink legal ribbon. Some of the documents had been sealed with bright red wax. None could doubt the holder of these papers.

The next step was to find accommodation that befitted his new status. Someone of such elevated descent would not set foot south of the river so our newly noble fellow had taken his luggage and slipped out of the lodging house to jump in a passing carriage. And in that short distance over the Bridge to the other side he left behind not only Gulliver Truepin and a host of other guises, but also a debt to the lodging house for, true to character (whichever one he was), he did not pay his bill.

Now, a week on, the self-satisfied swindler was enjoying the comfort of his new rooms and identity. He was immensely pleased with his transformation and could hardly take his eye off himself.

'But what accent shall I have?' he wondered as he sprayed his new, expensive citrus scent over himself. He fancied he needed something a little more exotic than usual. Perhaps he should amend his V's and W's.

'I haf alvays vanted to come to the City,' he said. He frowned. Too strong. Perhaps just the V. It was only to hint at his foreign provenance, after all, not to define him. He had other characteristics that would engage the ladies, said ladies being his preferred prey. (Their boredom and excessive money were usually a good combination for a practised con man.) His nose in profile might be long but from the front there was no doubting that he was actually quite an attractive fellow. And his lost eye always aroused much sympathy.

'Oh my!' he mimicked to the mirror in a high-pitched voice. 'Tell me, how did you come to lose it?'

He drew himself up to his full height (aided in this instance by custom-made heel inserts). On account of the scar through one eyebrow only the other moved, but at this point the action of that other more than compensated, and along with the furrowed brow gave an air of sincerity tinged with tragedy.

'Well, my dear,' he said deeply, taking a step back and resting his hand on his hip, 'it is a story I hesitate to recount . . . but if you insist, though you must be sure to tell me if you feel faint at the rather more horrific parts.'

And he practised again his tale of a lengthy duel over a Matter of Honour. A duel he had won in the end, of course.

The truth, as is often the case, was rather less exciting. As a peasant youth, still known then as Jereome, he had managed to trip over his bootlaces and land on a boar's tusk, thus rendering his eye irreparably damaged. But such a lowly story would not do any more. Besides, a man such as he now claimed to be would never wear anything as common as bootlaces!

Yawning widely, the fiendish trickster stretched and

disrobed, enjoying the feel of each item of clothing as he folded it carefully and put it away. He donned a soft embroidered nightshirt and a nightcap and before he climbed into bed he removed his false eye, gave it a little caress and placed it in a small velvet bag on his bedside table.

He reached into a drawer and took out a cutting from the *Northside Diurnal* (they too had paid *so* much more than he expected!). Although the recent downfall of Augustus Fitzbaudly still dominated the headlines, he was more interested in the society section. He turned the sheets until he came to a half-page illustration of dancing ladies and gentlemen, and read again the caption beneath the sketch:

> Northside Lords and Ladies of Urbs Umida enjoy
> the recent Vintners' Ball (ports and wines supplied
> by Faulkner's of Vine Street)

He stared at the picture with a wide grin. 'Soon, very soon,' he thought, 'that will be me.'

Chapter Nine

─── ───

The Landlord's Pickle

'A penny a go!' shouted Hector. 'A penny. Who today will challenge me with a riddle for a penny?'

Hector stood on a podium in the middle of Fiveways. He was well acquainted with the place these days. He was thinner than he used to be, and his clothes were more worn, but he was cheerful and energetic. His dark eyes scanned the small crowd that had gathered around him. Not so many this morning, but Hector knew there was always someone willing to part with a penny or two and soon the riddles came thick and fast.

'What can a man break many times without touching?'

'His promise,' replied Hector. 'Let's 'ave another.'

'Give me food and I will live; give me water and I will die. What am I?'

'Fire. Another.'

'What can a craftsman make that is never seen?'

'Noise,' said Hector. 'Any more?'

A large man stepped forward, his arms folded across his barrel-like chest. 'You won't get this one,' he said. 'I found it in a book!'

The crowd 'oohed' and 'aaahed' and applauded. Imagine, a book!

'We'll see,' said Hector evenly. He had found that those who were most sure of themselves were usually the losers. 'Let us hear it.'

'How does a man get down from an elephant?'

The crowd laughed. Some asked their neighbour, 'What's an elephant?'

Hector pretended to think, steepling his fingers and looking skyward. 'I believe,' he replied slowly, 'that you can't get down from an elephant because it comes only from a duck!'

The crowd cheered and clapped as Hector smiled broadly. Riddling, something that once had been little more than an enjoyable diversion with his father, was proving to be a lucrative skill. Sometimes he almost felt it was wrong to accept payment – he enjoyed the whole act so immensely, and it lifted for a while the sombre mood that had descended on him since losing his father. But Polly, who often stole a moment from her day and came down to hear Hector at work or bring him lunch, told him that was nonsense, that he thought about things far too much. As another penny landed at his feet, he bent to pick it up and a new voice cut through the noise.

'Hi, young man! I have a riddle for you.'

Hector looked around. He couldn't see to whom the voice belonged.

'And what is it, sir?' he called out. He spotted a figure in the mob surrounding him. On account of his odd-shaped hat, his face was obscured. He sounded older than Hector but not yet a full-grown man.

'It is called the Landlord's Pickle,' said the stranger, 'and it goes thus:

> Ten weary footsore travellers,
>   All in a woeful plight,
> Sought shelter at a wayside inn
>   One dark and stormy night.

"Nine rooms, no more," the landlord said
"Have I to offer you,
To each of eight a single bed,
But the ninth must serve for two."

A din arose. The troubled host
Could only scratch his head,
For of those tired men no two
Would occupy one bed.

The puzzled host was soon at ease –
He was a clever man –
And so to please his guests devised
This most ingenious plan.'

The fellow stopped for a moment. 'And this is the puzzle,'
he called up to Hector before concluding the rhyme:

'Here I stop 'fore riddle's end
To ask, young friend of mine,
How did that landlord please his guests,
And fit ten into nine?'

Hector pursed his lips and looked thoughtful. Ten into nine? This was not a riddle he had come across. He would have expected it from his father, not from a member of this crowd. It wasn't that southsiders lacked intelligence, but what intelligence they had was not necessarily suited to riddling.

'I'll need some time for this one,' said Hector.

'Take all the time you need. Tell me the answer when next we meet,' came the reply.

'When will that be?' asked Hector. 'Tomorrow?'

'Perhaps,' was all the stranger said, and, still obscured by the crowd, he began to walk away.

The crowd was as curious as Hector. 'So what is the answer?' shouted up a regular.

'*Tempus omnia revelat*,' said Hector, reverting unthinkingly to his previous persona before realizing no one knew what he was talking about.

'He means, *Time will tell*,' came a shout, and Hector just caught sight of the back of the mysterious riddler's head as he disappeared down one of the alleys.

'Yes, time will tell,' he murmured.

Now it was snowing. Sensing that riddling was over for today his audience moved away. Hector stepped down, the pennies clinking in his purse. Some, of course, would be given to Mrs Fitch, and the remainder he would keep for himself. He went to the nearest food stall and took shelter with a hot potato and a mug of mulled ale, lost in melancholy thoughts.

In the six weeks since he had arrived at Fitch's, summer – characterized by a rise in temperature and a proportional increase in strength of stench from the Foedus – was over and autumn, in this city merely a couple of weeks of cooler weather, was fast giving way to winter.

It had been a difficult time for Hector but he had done his best to adjust to this radical change in lifestyle. There were twenty other boys at the home, all natives of the south side and all orphaned by Fate, often in the form of gin. The first morning at breakfast Hector was greeted with suspicion, as any newcomer would be. Then as soon as he spoke he was identified as a northerner and a fight immediately ensued. Hector fell at the second punch – he was no match for his tough streetwise housemates. As he lay on the floor wondering how he could possibly come out of this alive, he noticed through his rapidly swelling eye that one of the boys was wearing his coat and hat and another his boots and watch. Quick as a flash, he pulled out his cocoon and reminded them of that night when they had helped themselves to his belongings.

As soon as Hector's identity was established the leader (the same fellow from the night he had been robbed) called a halt to the conflict. The little lad, still wearing the cravat (now rather darker in colour than it had once been), helped Hector to his feet and begged him to retell the riddle of the liar for they all still failed to grasp the solution. Hector obliged, more than once, and henceforth was held in high regard as a fellow of learning and an entertainer. Polly's belief in his survival instincts had been proved right. But he still had to find a way to get on outside the Home's doors.

Deducing early on in his stay at Fitch's that the prevailing accent was basically a matter of dropped aitches and ripe expletives, Hector adjusted his own accent accordingly. Within a week it was almost as if he had never spoken any other way. Occasionally the odd 'By Jove!' or 'Splendid, old chap!' or Latin expletive slipped out – old habits die hard – causing the boys to look at him askance and laugh, but it wasn't long before some of his new companions, in homage to Hector, started to use the expressions themselves.

But what endeared Hector to them most was when he posed riddles or read to them – the humorous verses of

Beag Hickory, or sometimes, at Polly's particular insistence, magical stories from *Houndsecker's Tales of Faeries and Blythe Spirits*, a copy of which one of the boys had 'acquired' from an unsuspecting bookseller in the City.

So life at Lottie's was not as unpleasant as Hector had first imagined it might be. He was fed, he had shelter and he could earn money riddling. The jobs the other boys did to this end were many and varied. Some crossed the Bridge and polished gentlemen's shoes, others swept the crossings or just begged, and needless to say they all thieved. Hector was not much of a pickpocket, so at first he had sold chicken feet door to door, but now he had his riddling.

As long as you said grace before meals, joined Mrs Fitch in prayer whenever the feeling took her (often), sang her hymns when she sang them (often and loudly) and carried out basic chores, then your life was your own. Yes, he had to put up with lice and fleas and foul smells and the danger on the streets, but this was traded for freedom. He hadn't forgotten the long dreary days in the schoolroom with his tutor, conjugating his verbs and declining his nouns, ever wary of the cane with which his tutor seemed particularly free and easy.

But when darkness fell each evening, so too did his

mood. He missed his father sorely and inside anger and an increasing desire for revenge were eating away at his heart. And he was heavily burdened by the weight of his secret past. He didn't dare tell Lottie his family name, not now that it was blackened by its association with gin. She would have him out on the street! It was during these dark hours that Polly came to his rescue. Her cheerful and non-prying nature usually brought him round.

Hector took every opportunity, day and night, to search for Truepin. He knew in his heart that he was probably gone from the City, but he had to believe that one day he would right the terrible wrongs that had been done to his family. Often he would return late at night, cold and hungry, but Polly, who was always up and waiting for him, never said a word or enquired about his whereabouts, only fed him and put him to bed. Other times, when Hector sat with her at the kitchen table and helped her with her letters and penmanship, she would look at him quizzically, as if inviting him to answer the unasked question, but he never did.

Only once did she say something. It was after midnight and Hector was slumped across the table, pale and exhausted.

'Hector,' Polly began gently, 'I don't know who or what you seek these winter nights, and I don't want to know, but

I can see that it is doing you no good at all.'

Hector opened his mouth to protest but she put up her hand to silence him.

'I'm your friend. I hate to see you like this. Sometimes you just have to leave the past behind otherwise it will eat you up.'

Hector knew she was right. If only I could just forget it all, he thought. But in his mind's eye he saw again his father's lifeless body in the butterfly house and he knew he had to continue to the bitter end, wherever it lay.

Chapter Ten

BEWARE

CITIZENS OF URBS UMIDA

THE DEVIL'S SWEAT

THIS VILE LIQUID, THIS JUNIPER POISON, SENT
BY BEELZEBUB HIMSELF TO TEMPT US FROM
THE PATH OF RIGHTEOUSNESS, LEADS ONLY TO
WICKED ENTERPRISE AND REMOVES ALL SENSE
OF SHAME AND IMBECILLITATES ONE AND ALL

✴ *DO NOT SUCCUMB!!!* ✴

I, LOTTIE FITCH, AM LIVING PROOF THAT IT NEED
NOT BE SO. YES, I HAVE DRUNK THE DEVIL'S SWEAT
AND TAKEN PLEASURE IN ITS SWEET LETHARGY
AND CONSEQUENTIAL DISCOMBOBULATIONS

✴ *BUT NO LONGER* ✴

WITH THE HELP OF THE DIVINE I HAVE OVERCOME MY
POISONOUS HABIT, THIS MIND-ALTERING ADDICTION
THAT LED ME ONLY TO CRUELTY AND ABUSE

AND SO TOO CAN YOU

The Devil's Sweat

Lottie Fitch put down the leaflet and took a moment to herself in the kitchen. She still had cravings, strongest in the morning, for the gin that had been her master for so many years, but she put her hands together and prayed with all her might for the strength to resist. She ran her tongue around her mouth and felt the teeth – and gaps – within. She thought of Hector and his fine set of teeth and it caused her to smile sadly.

Hector's arrival, near two months ago, had made Lottie think more of her own son, Ludlow. He would have been Hector's age the last time she saw him. It pained her new-found conscience greatly to think how she and Ned had so cruelly driven him away. She hardly blamed him for going. They had not been fit parents by any manner of means. So much of Lottie's previous life was just a blur that she even had trouble recalling exactly what Ludlow looked like. He had brown eyes, hadn't he? Or were they green? She could ask Ned. No, he probably wouldn't know either. If Lottie's mind was rather addled, his was ten times worse. He had certainly out-drunk her down the years.

For most of her life, like many Urbs Umidians, God and his mysterious ways were of little interest to Lottie. But that distant winter's night when her other half (neither better nor worse) Ned fell in the Foedus proved to be a life-changing moment for the two of them. They had arrived at the river that snowy evening simply because they were in desperate pursuit of their son, Ludlow. If truth be told, they were trying to sell his teeth. Ludlow was not at all keen to be caught, not only because his teeth were still in his head, but also because he had no illusions about his place in his parents' affections – somewhere after gin and money. The chase culminated in Ludlow's wrestling for his life with his father on the river bank. Ned lost his grip and fell in the Foedus and Ludlow escaped.

As soon as Ned's head slipped under Lottie wailed and

screamed, as was expected, but other than that accepted his demise rather rapidly. Fortunately for Ned people had gathered around at the commotion and, wouldn't you know, one of them had a rope. He tossed it to Ned who, more by luck than design, managed to grab it. He was then hauled ashore.

'I can't feel my legs,' he had groaned as he was dragged up the bank. Lottie didn't believe him and kicked him sharply in the shins but he didn't so much as flinch. In all probability they were numb from the freezing water but that didn't explain why he hadn't walked since that day. Lottie had been disappointed at this outcome, namely his survival, but the cries of 'It's a miracle!' and 'God be praised!' from the assembled crowd had struck a chord with her and it was at that very moment, on the snowy banks of the Foedus, that she had her first vision.

There appeared in front of her the ghostly shape of a young child on his knees. He was crying, his thin arms outstretched searching for food in the snow, and Lottie was suddenly and unexpectedly moved to tears. In fact the child was not a vision, but flesh and bone, just particularly pale. In the crush of the crowd he had dropped a hot chestnut, which was immediately trodden underfoot, and he was scrabbling for it.

Lottie turned away to see Ned being dragged off to the Nimble Finger, a haunt of his, for a warming drink by the fire, and when she looked back the boy was gone. She thought to follow his ghostly footprints in the snow and eventually came to Hookstone Row, some five or six streets away from the river. The footsteps led directly to a large abandoned house crawling with orphaned boys. As she stood in the doorway and saw their dirty faces looking hopefully at hers, Lottie felt even more profoundly the very recent loss of her own son and vowed to come to the aid of these unfortunates. And thus was founded Lottie Fitch's Home for Exposed Babies and Abandoned Boys.

Whether or not there had been divine intervention that evening, at least one miracle had occurred: Lottie was a changed woman. She immediately gave up the Juniper Water and threw herself into her new role as mother to the waifs and strays of Urbs Umida. Ned, still numb of leg when he moved in also, had not given up gin but, out of respect for Lottie, he pretended he had and had it smuggled in by numerous friends who came to visit him in his new home. What Lottie don't know don't cause 'er no 'arm, he thought, and from then on the Fitches coexisted quite happily, Ned at the top of the house and Lottie, in the main, downstairs.

Having renounced her vice, Lottie spent much of her day on the streets proclaiming loudly the evils of drink and handing out her leaflets. And it was on these same streets that she came across Polly. Down on her luck and in despair, Polly was about to try a cup of the beguiling liquid from a gin pipe. Lottie intervened just in time and enlisted her to help out in the kitchen at the Home.

When Lottie found out that Polly had known Ludlow in Pagus Parvus she was astounded, worried and pleased at the same time, which was quite a challenge to her shrivelled brain – astounded at the coincidence, worried that Ludlow might have told Polly how badly she and Ned had treated their son (he hadn't) and ultimately pleased that he was alive and well. The good Lord, in one of her many daily visions, told Lottie that one day they would be reunited. Until then, she was content to carry on as before.

And so it had been for nearly six years.

Lottie's thoughts turned back to Hector. He was proving a useful addition to Fitch's Home, she reflected; willing, reliable and entertaining. He was different from the other boys, there was no denying that – he was a northsider after all. But despite the differences Hector had settled in quickly enough. He might not be much good with his fists but he had proved there were more ways than one to skin a cat. And Lottie had not failed to notice how Polly had taken the boy under her wing.

Lottie came out of her reverie and went upstairs to take her cloak from a peg in the hall. Her pockets were full of corks (for plugging up the gin pipes) and her bag was stuffed with leaflets. She liked to stand on the Bridge and ask for money to support her boys. To this end she always took a couple of the younger ones along, the two with particularly morose expressions. She had asked Hector once – Lord knows he looked miserable enough sometimes – but he had refused.

'Too soft, 'e is,' she sighed. 'Took 'is pa's death very hard. But a good boy nonetheless.'

As Lottie came down the steps to the street she saw a figure standing across the road. She thought he might be smiling at her but it was hard to tell with all the people passing by. He had a bag over his shoulder and wore a hat of unusual design. She was certain he was the same fellow who had been there the day before and the day before that. She blinked and he was gone.

Chapter Eleven

Article from

The Northside Diurnal Journal

A quality daily newspaper for the discerning reader

Honoured Guests at Wine Emporium Opening

By

Tarquin Faulkner

Lady Lysandra Mandible (pictured above), dressed in an assortment of white fur, looked simply exquisite when she made a guest appearance at the opening of the third branch of Faulkner's Wine Emporium.

Lady Mandible was accompanied by Baron Bovrik de Vandolin (also pictured). It has not taken this exotic and enigmatic Baron long to endear himself to Urbs Umidian high society. Since arriving in the City some weeks ago this charming man (a member of the Eastern European branch of the noble de Vandolin family) has proved a highly popular and much sought after dinner, dance and party guest. He has an enviable reputation as a most entertaining fellow of great wit and imagination, and he is also a hero. Who has not heard the tragic story of the loss of his left eye in a duel over a slighted woman? But Baron Bovrik de Vandolin is not the sort of fellow to allow such an optical inconvenience to hold him back.

As for Lady Mandible herself, she hardly needs an introduction. Without doubt the most beautiful and talented lady to ever have graced the corridors of Withypitts Hall, the Mandible family seat, she has a reputation not only for style and taste but also for her extravagant nature, and we northsiders love her for it! It is believed that no expense was spared in her recent renovation of Withypitts Hall. No doubt all will be revealed at the Mandible Annual Midwinter Feast.

Since the tragic death of his father last year, young Lord Mandible is rarely in the City, preferring to stay within the confines of Withypitts, some six hours' ride away. He has never been particularly fond of dancing or parties on account of his withered leg and no doubt he is pleased that Baron Bovrik accompanies Lady Mandible to all society functions in the City.

Despite the fact that many young ladies of the City are purported to be under the Baron's spell, he is immune to their charms and dedicated to the task set before him. Of course, it is common knowledge that he has been charged with helping to organize the Mandible Midwinter Feast. We northsider Urbs Umidians look forward to it with great anticipation. Always a marvellous occasion, one feels this year that Lady Mandible will make it her own.

Hector put the crumpled page down on the floor beside his mattress and leaned over to trace with his finger for the hundredth time Baron Bovrik de Vandolin's profile. Then he settled back with a frown.

'What a master of deception you are, Truepin,' he murmured, rolling his ebony cocoon between his fingers. For, if this sketch was accurate, there was little doubt in Hector's mind that Gulliver Truepin and Bovrik de Vandolin were one and the same.

'And if you aren't,' he said out loud, 'at the very least I owe it to Father to find out.'

Chapter Twelve

A Disturbing Encounter

Hector pressed himself tightly to the wall and cautiously peered around the corner at the gleaming black carriage that had just drawn up in the street. Despite his outward appearance of calm, his heart was thumping wildly behind his ribs. He watched as the driver jumped down and opened the door. The passenger, a man, was holding a brass-tipped and handled cane which tapped smartly on the pavement. Hector noticed how the toes of his shoes, sporting large gold buckles, gleamed. Suddenly the wind took the man's cloak and whipped it open to reveal beneath an unusual palette: yellow ochre breeches with darker satin ties and a waistcoat of peridot green. He stood for a moment, admiring his reflection in the window, then pulled at the patch over his left eye and tweaked his waxed moustache before walking into the building.

The driver's back was turned so Hector slipped along the pavement and crept up to the door. He sniffed, his senses alerted. Could he smell citrus? His lip curled when he read the names on the glass before him: Badlesmire and Leavelund, Solicitors and Auctioneers.

A combination of luck and intuition had brought him here. The *Diurnal Journal* tracked Lady Mandible's — and therefore the Baron's — every move. Thanks also to the journal Hector knew where they stayed when in the City: Lady Mandible's town house. Hector had kept a close watch on the house all day. As evening fell his patience was rewarded. The front door opened and a man emerged. He set off at a quick pace towards the river. Hector was quite certain this man was Bovrik de Vandolin, but the real question was, could he also be Gulliver Truepin? From this distance and in this light he just couldn't be sure. He followed cautiously all the way to the Bridge at which point Bovrik hailed a carriage. Hector heard him say, 'Roebemlynde Street,' and off he went.

Although Hector was on foot he had no trouble keeping

up. It was market day, and the streets were crammed with cattle and pigs and street sellers; besides, he knew the narrow short cuts where the carriage couldn't go, so he was already waiting in Roebemlynde Street when the carriage arrived.

Despite the fact that they were sited south of the river, Badlesmire and Leavelund's client list had more than its fair share of well-off northsiders. Their sign might read 'solicitors and auctioneers', but everyone knew they had their greedy fingers in many pies. It was the place to go if you had a problem, legal or otherwise, and you didn't want your neighbours to know what you were up to. They were happy too to act as middlemen in the buying and selling of goods they might serendipitously encounter in the course of their business.

Frustrated that he hadn't yet had a good look at the man, Hector went back round the corner, scaled the wall at the side and jumped down into a small yard behind the offices. He positioned himself on a discarded tea chest under the window. He could see the three men within and hear their loud, self-congratulatory conversation.

'Ah, Baron de Vandolin,' purred Badlesmire, a large man with fat fingers. 'Mr Leavelund and I have been expecting you.' Leavelund, quite the opposite in build to his partner, was standing just behind him, rubbing his bony hands and drawing his lips back over his long teeth as if trying to dislodge something stuck between them.

'Is it ready?' asked Bovrik in a slightly Germanic accent.

'Yes, yes,' said Leavelund. 'All packed and ready to go. An excellent purchase, I must say. Shame about the owner, of course.'

'There is no excuse for stupidity,' remarked Bovrik coldly, his one eye glaring.

'Well, it's an ill wind . . .' chipped in Badlesmire. 'Mr Fitzbaudley's troubles have kept us busy. It's a complicated thing to wrap up a failing business, you understand. We have disposed of everything at this stage. But as soon as we heard you and Lady Mandible were interested in this –' he glanced at a crate on the table –'we set it aside.'

Bovrik nodded with obvious satisfaction.

'And you, Baron, do you have the other thing we discussed?' continued Badlesmire.

'I haf indeed,' replied Bovrik, and he produced from under his cloak a gleaming white marble statuette of a Grecian water bearer. Both the solicitors smiled broadly and fussed noisily over it.

For though Hector did not yet know it, Bovrik, true to form and in accordance with his plan, was making good money on the side selling various valuables from Withypitts Hall. Only ones that Lady Mandible wouldn't miss, of course, and there were so many trinkets in the place it had to be impossible to keep track. Besides, she was always changing things around and getting rid of discrete items. He was merely taking advantage of her whims for once rather than pandering to them.

As Leavelund put the statuette away, Hector watched Badlesmire take a bottle and three glasses from a cupboard.

'We also had to clear Fitzbaudly's cellar,' he said conversationally. 'Some very rare vintages down there. And of course the hours and hours of work we put in – well, there wasn't even a penny left over after the bill was paid. Fitzbaudly himself is dead now of course. From shame, no doubt.'

'I belief it's Fitz*badly*,' said Bovrik dryly and the three of them shared a laugh and a glass of Chateau Huit du Pipe '56.

Outside Hector clenched his fists and tried vainly to suppress his growing fury. The scent in the doorway, the

Fitzbadly joke, the eyepatch and the nose; now he knew for sure. Bovrik de Vandolin *was* Gulliver Truepin. Even his fake Germanic accent and his popinjay clothes couldn't disguise him any longer. As for the crate, whatever was in it could only be something that had once belonged to his father, which fact only served to infuriate him further. He watched until the three men drained their glasses and shook hands then he returned to the street corner just in time to see the Baron emerge with flushed cheeks and a very self-satisfied look on his face. He tapped his cane impatiently on the pavement as the driver loaded his new crate awkwardly on to the carriage roof.

'Careful, my man,' he called irritably in his clipped voice. 'There's glass in there.'

All those nights under the stairs, thought Hector, lying awake thinking what he would do when next he saw Truepin, the cruel instrument of his father's misfortune and now finally, here he was, only feet away. Hector felt a rage well up from the pit of his stomach and everything around him faded until all he could see was Bovrik de Vandolin.

Time seemed to slow as he began to walk towards the Baron. He didn't know what he was going to do, or how, but he flexed his fingers and gritted his teeth until it hurt.

Bovrik, sensing that he was no longer alone, turned around. He narrowed his one good eye and sneered with contempt at the audacity of this urchin who dared approach him. Then, just as Hector was almost upon him, something fluttered out of the carriage and landed on Bovrik's sleeve. He looked down at it and raised his hand as if to swat it away.

'No!' cried Hector, stopping in his tracks. 'Don't!'

Bovrik lowered his hand and looked at Hector.

'It's only a moth,' he said. 'Why should I not kill it?'

Hector was breathing fast, and he could feel his face burning. The rage within was still fierce but he suddenly knew now was not the time.

'It's not a moth,' he said as calmly as he could manage. 'It's a butterfly. *Thecla betulae*.'

'A butterfly? But it is nearly winter.'

'It must have been sheltering in the carriage,' said Hector, and carefully he lifted it on to his hand. Bovrik flinched at his touch and shook his sleeve distastefully. Then his expression changed. 'Do you know about butterflies?'

'Yes,' said Hector stiffly. 'I know all about them.'

Bovrik pursed his lips. 'How fortunate. I am in need of a butterfly expert. Haf you heard of Lady Mandible of Withypitts Hall?'

Hector nodded. He could feel himself gradually calming down, the fierce heat behind his eyes subsiding. He could hardly believe he had come so close to trying to harm the man. What was he thinking! In broad daylight (admittedly more *grey*light than daylight this side of the river) in the middle of the street outside a solicitors'! He must have been temporarily insane.

'Her Ladyship, Lady Mandible, has asked me to procure for her some butterflies for the Midwinter Feast,' continued Bovrik. 'Is it something you could do?'

'I believe I could,' said Hector slowly. This was an unexpected turn of events. He could use it to his advantage.

'Then come to Withypitts. I'll send a carriage for you.'

Hector nodded and he could feel the last of his anger slowly dissipating, and a plan taking its place.

The driver, having finally managed to secure the crate, indicated that it was time to go. Bovrik stepped up quickly into the carriage. He leaned out of the window.

'And your name, boy?' he asked as he handed Hector a note, telling him where to wait for the carriage and when.

'Hector Fi—'. He stopped abruptly. What sort of fool was he to tell Bovrik his surname! He hoped the Baron hadn't noticed his hesitation.

'Just Hector.'

And then as he watched the carriage trundle away a hand reached out of the window and flung something on the ground. It rolled unevenly to Hector and he picked it up. A penny.

'Your treachery will cost you far more than this,' said Hector. 'Far, far, more.'

Chapter Thirteen

A Difficult Journey

The sun was already low in the sky as Hector stood outside the Nimble Finger stamping his feet and rubbing his hands together. People were saying that it was going to be a bad winter. They still talked about when the Foedus had frozen over. Hector remembered it too. He was five and his father had taken him to have a look. He had thought the river would be white but instead the frozen water was dark grey. Opportunistic merchants had set up their stalls, fires were burning, chestnuts were roasting, the atmosphere was merry and noisy. Of course Hector had wanted to go on to the ice but his father would not allow it, so he could only watch from the bank. Hector remembered the expression

F. E. Higgins

on his father's face as he observed the people moving to and
fro below. He had the queerest feeling that he too wished
he could be down there with them.

The sound of clattering hoofs and turning wheels rudely
interrupted Hector's thoughts. A carriage drew up.

''Ector?' called the driver. 'For Withypitts?'

'Yes, I am he,' said Hector.

'I'm Solomon,' said the driver, peering closely at Hector.
The boy's clothes were tatty, yes, but the way he spoke, like
a native but not quite, and the air he had about him . . .
There's more to this dark-eyed boy than first appears, he
thought. And why should a baron send a carriage for him?

'How long will it take?' asked Hector as he climbed in.

'Oooh,' said Solomon, knitting his brows and sucking
air in through his teeth. 'Depends, you see, on the weather,
the roads. Been a lot of rain recently, might be snow later.
I reckon as we'll stop off on the way, small place I know
further into the mountains, a village, makes the journey
shorter, though much later in the year that way's impassable
with the snow.'

'Very well,' said Hector, and he shut the door and settled
on the seat. He heard the crack of a whip, there was a jolt
and then he was off, rattling down the road away from Urbs

90

Umida, from Polly and Lottie and from his father.

It was not a comfortable ride; the seats were distinctly less well padded than those he had once known but, having learned recently that it was possible to get used to almost anything, Hector resigned himself to it. He felt as if he was leaving behind not just one life but two, that of south and north.

Soon evening swallowed the daylight and he pulled the carriage curtain closed. His thoughts turned to Bovrik and his mind filled to the brim with murderous thoughts that set his heart racing. But he smiled through his clenched teeth. The irony of the situation didn't escape him. That Janus-faced fraud, he thought grimly, has brought about his own end by inviting me to him.

They were climbing now and the temperature was dropping. Hector pulled his father's cloak tighter and succumbed to the fatigue that had been building all day. The cloak, and the cocoon around his neck, were the only two things he had to remember his father by.

A bone-shaking jolt woke Hector from a deep sleep and threw him to the floor. '*Tartri flammis!*' he exclaimed, and sat back down bracing himself with his hands, only for another violent jerk to unseat him. The driver's fears were well founded; the recent storms had wreaked havoc with the roads.

Without warning there was a tremendous thud, an ear-splitting crack and a terrible tearing sound. The carriage veered sharply to the left and toppled over to land on its side. When all was still Hector, shaken but unharmed, managed to stand up. He retrieved his bag and crawled out of the door, which was now above his head, and saw Solomon standing on the side of the road cursing and swearing.

'We've lost a wheel,' he said as he unharnessed the horses. 'But the village is a short distance up ahead. We can 'ave the carriage repaired there before setting off again.'

So, in the eerie glow of the gibbous moon, to the rhythmic accompaniment of the horses' hoofs, Hector and Solomon rode in parallel up the steep hill. Soon they saw the lights of the village and Hector noted a large flat-faced stone at the side of the road upon which were etched the words 'Pagus Parvus'.

'*Pagus Parvus*,' murmured Hector. 'Small village.' His tutor of old would have been pleased.

'We can get some 'elp here,' said Solomon, sounding relieved. 'And 'ave an 'ot meal.'

Hector looked up the moonlit street. The hill was almost

impossibly steep and he imagined the villagers having to pull themselves up by the window ledges just to get safely from one end to the other. They dismounted outside a tavern, the Pickled Trout, and handed the horses over to the care of a young boy who had run out upon hearing them. Hector followed Solomon into the tavern to be met with a burst of warm air and the sound of laughter. The landlord was polishing, or at least wiping, a glass behind the bar when he saw the two visitors. 'Solomon!' he called out. 'You're most welcome, sir!'

'Benjamin Tup!' Solomon hailed in return. He made his way to the bar and explained briefly about the carriage and Benjamin immediately organized a couple of men to go to repair it. 'What's your pleasure?' he asked the two of them.

'Ale, for me and young 'Ector 'ere ,' said Solomon, 'and let's 'ave some stew while you're at it.'

Solomon took his drink and went to a table by the wall, slopping his overfull jug on the sawdust-covered floor. He seemed a popular fellow and was hailed heartily left, right and centre. Hector joined him and an old woman came over to greet them. She had a nervous tic that caused her to wink intermittently.

'So, where are you two off to tonight?' she asked.

'To Withypitts Hall,' said Hector.

Hector didn't know if he had spoken particularly loudly or if perhaps he had chosen a moment when the room was particularly quiet, but as soon as the words left his mouth the entire room went silent.

'It's a strange sort of place for a young lad,' remarked the old lady.

'I hope to be employed by Lady Mandible for the Midwinter Feast,' Hector explained. 'But what is so strange about Withypitts Hall?'

'Not so much the Hall,' said Benjamin, crossing his arms and leaning forward on the bar, 'as the inhabitants! The comings and goings from that place! Lady Mandible's deliveries pass through the village all the time and you've never seen the like. A trunk fell from a cart once, split in two, and the contents scattered all over the road. Little statuettes and ornaments of hideous creatures. Stuffed animals – I couldn't put a name to 'em – and bones, big and small. Now what would a lady want with such outlandish objects?'

All those listening murmured in agreement.

'Off to Withypitts, eh?' said a man, stepping out of the

shadows. 'I'll tell you a story that'll really make you think twice about going there.'

'Very well,' said Hector. 'But I warn you, I am not easily swayed from my purpose.'

Neither, it seemed, was the man. He sat at the table and began.

'My name is Oscar Carpue. I too hail from Urbs Umida and it was in that city I was framed, by my own father-in-law, for a murder I did not commit. I couldn't risk waiting for the constables. I was a poor man, he was rich. What hope had I of proving my innocence? So I too fled, leaving my young son, Pin, behind, and I came to Pagus Parvus. I went back to find him as soon as I could risk it, but he was gone from our lodgings. How I miss him still.

'As for Withypitts Hall, I hardly wish to return there either. We villagers pay little heed to the goings-on at that place. But we heard that Lord Mandible's son married, and then soon after that old Lord Mandible himself died. More recently rumours reached us of a one-eyed man who had been taken on by Lady Mandible. When, a couple of weeks ago, a gleaming black carriage with scarlet blinds and three attendants rode into the village we knew this was the infamous Baron Bovrik de Vandolin.

'He was seeking a carpenter and, as that is my trade, I went to Withypitts. It's an odd place to behold, constructed from huge blocks of dark mountain rock with much decorative stonework. If you look for long enough you see that there are creatures hiding in the carvings: fierce griffins and hideous gargoyles. The porch pillars conceal lizards and snakes in their flowering capitals. It leaves you feeling that you are always observed.

'I set to work immediately in the great dining hall, preparing it for the Midwinter Feast. My tasks were straightforward: repairing the panelled walls, securing loose floorboards, levelling the chairs. I saw hardly a soul in my time there, but above the sound of my lathe and hammer I often heard Lord Mandible and his two cats at the harpsichord.

'One evening, just after the clock struck ten, I heard a great commotion from elsewhere in the building. I am as curious as the next man so I laid down my tools and followed the noise to the entrance hall where I saw a most peculiar sight. A party of men, huntsmen by their garb, was standing over a creature of some sort laid out on the marble floor. It was large and dark-haired with four limbs – what I would consider both legs *and* arms in the manner of an ape –

and an enormous skull. Its smell was pungent, of rotting meat, as if it was already dead. But as I watched I saw its chest rise and fall. It moved suddenly and a huntsman stuck a dagger up to the hilt in its side. It moaned and turned its head and I swear it looked straight into my eyes. Even now I cannot describe to you how it made me feel.

'I gathered from the conversation that the creature had been captured in the nearby oak forest. At first the men thought they were trailing a Hairy-Backed Hog. It was only when they shot and injured it that they realized they had something quite different. I wanted to step forward, to offer the creature some comfort, but then Bovrik and Lady Mandible suddenly appeared.

'"It could be of scientific interest," said one huntsman.

'"We should keep it alive," said another, "and send it to the City for examination."

'"Sell it to a freak show," suggested a third.

'Lady Mandible's expression seemed to indicate that she thought little of these suggestions. "If it was captured in the forest, then it belongs to me," she said, "so I will decide its fate." And something about the tone of her voice and the way Bovrik's lips curled into a sneering smile made my skin crawl. I crept away before I was discovered.

'I finished the job as fast as I could. I desired now only to leave, and a week later I collected my money and departed. As I walked away down the hill a large cart came towards me, on the back of which was a wooden crate. The cart hit a pothole, narrowly avoiding overturning, but the crate slid sharply forward and one side flew open. The driver, cursing loudly, jumped down to secure the load.

'"For the Hall?" I asked as I went to help.

'"Aye," he replied. "And Lady Mandible will be right furious if it is damaged."

'With what I had heard and seen of the lady I was intrigued as to the crate's contents so I pulled away the broken side to look within. Had I known what I was to see I would never have done so.

'At first glance I saw only a chair. But I realized quickly that this was no ordinary chair.

'*It was the curious beast fashioned into a chair.*

'The arms of the chair were the beast's arms, its hands – for they were not paws – curled over the ends. The chair legs were the beast's forelegs and its feet – complete with toes – the chair's feet. The creature's skin was stretched over the seat and up the back and down again on the other side. The black fur was glossy and brushed all in the same direction. And, if I was still in any doubt, it was dispelled when I saw across the taut skin the scar of the huntsman's dagger. Hardly able to breathe from shock and revulsion, I silently thanked the Lord there was no head, for my heaving stomach could not have borne that. I learned later that it had been mounted as a trophy.

'I shall never forget the way that creature looked at me as he lay dying on the floor. For although it was not the face of a human I looked upon, I swear neither was its gaze that of a beast.'

— Part the Second —

The Hairy-Backed Forest Hog

The Hairy-Backed Forest Hog was given its name on account of the ridge of coarse black fur that runs the length of its spine. The legend goes that the Devil came up from Hell one day looking for a pig to roast. He wandered the vast oak forests that covered the land and just as night fell he came across a large hog rooting for nuts. Lacking a hunting spear the Devil threw his white-hot pitchfork at the hog in an attempt to kill it. His aim was off the mark and as the pitchfork fell a single tine grazed the hog's back and set him on fire. The hog ran squealing to the river and immersed itself but the water was not deep enough to cover the creature fully and the hair along its back was scorched.

When the hair grew back it was thick and black from the hog's neck to its tail and has been ever since.

The Hairy-Backed Forest Hog is found only in the ancient oak forest to the south-east of the Moiraean Mountains. These savage beasts mate for life and are fiercely protective of each other. The hog lives on a diet of acorns during the *late summer and autumn, supplementing them in winter with the fungus 'Stipitis longi', an underground mushroom which it sniffs out with its specially adapted nose.*

It is noteworthy that the hog eats only the harmless head of the fungus, leaving the fatally poisonous stalk in the ground.'

From **Myths and Folklore, Flora and Fauna of the Ancient Oak Forest**
Various authors c.1652

Chapter Fourteen

~

Extract from

A Letter to Polly

Dear Polly,

As I walk daily the maze-like corridors of Withy-pitts Hall, the smell of money is overpowering. The excess in which I now live, far greater than any I experienced in Urbs Umida, has to be seen to be believed.

I have always felt guilty that I left Fitch's without saying goodbye to you or any of the others. But my urgency was spurred on by anger. I don't know if you will ever read these letters. I address them to you, but in many ways I write them for myself. It helps to see it in black and white in front of me. It is my record, so when I look back on all of this I will know what I really felt and what drove me.

Father advised against revenge before he died. I know you would too, if you could. That is what you were counselling, that night in the kitchen. But I cannot agree. Baron Bovrik de Vandolin, under whatever guise or name, is a monster. Perhaps he did not deliver the fatal blow to my father, but I will always hold him responsible for his death. They hang at Gallows Corner for lesser crimes than his.

But enough! There is so much more to tell.

It was late by the time the carriage was fixed, so Solomon decided we would stay the night in Pagus Parvus, setting off again early the next day.

The old woman, Perigoe was her name, gave me another wink. 'If you will go to Withypitts,' she said, 'then I ask a favour. I am a bookseller, you see, and I have an order of books for Lady Mandible. Young Sourdough, my delivery boy, refuses to set foot there again since he heard Oscar's story.'

I consented readily and in return she offered me a room for the night.

For all my bravado and resolve I admit that I was unsettled by Oscar's tale and happy to delay our departure. I followed her out on to the street. Her bookshop was not far and I was glad to get out of the cold. But as I shut the door behind me I thought I saw a movement from across the street. Was someone watching?

'What is it?' Perigoe asked.

I looked again but there was nothing. 'Only a shadow,' I said, but I wasn't at all sure.

Perigoe's hospitality was first rate and I would have spent a very comfortable night in her attic room if my dreams hadn't been plagued with images of the beast.

Luck was against me. All next day we suffered a terrible storm. Solomon sent word from the Pickled Trout (where he had spent the night) that we would set off when it eased. The howling wind and lashing rain battered the village until late afternoon. It was frustrating but Perigoe looked after me. And I took the opportunity to browse her bookshop. I saw on the shelves many books from my own library – no doubt all disposed of by now thanks to Badlesmire and his rawboned partner – which saddened me. But my heart lifted to see a slim volume of poetry by Beag Hickory. Another book too caught my eye: 'Myths and Folklore, Flora and Fauna of the Ancient Oak Forest'. I bought it though Perigoe kindly charged me a reduced price. I had a feeling it might be useful.

By early evening the storm had abated and Solomon arrived with the repaired carriage. He was anxious to go, not so much to reach my destination as to be able to return to the City. Perigoe gave me a warm hug and handed over a parcel of books wrapped in oilcloth and tied with string for Lady Mandible. (She told me the lady orders some odd titles.) As a parting gift she gave me the copy of Beag Hickory's poetry. Her kindness made me forget my inner darkness for a moment, at least.

'Look out for yourself,' warned Perigoe. 'Lady Mandible is not one to be crossed. She has a silver smile, they say, but a hand of steel in a velvet glove.'

I didn't care about Lady Mandible, though, only Baron Bovrik. I climbed into the carriage and Solomon opened the hatch to look down at me with bleary bloodshot eyes. 'Are you sure you want to go on?' he asked gruffly. 'I can always take you back to the City.'

I thought of Father buried in a shallow pauper's grave.

'Yes,' I said. 'I'm sure.'

Solomon had assured me that we would reach Withypitts Hall in a matter of hours. To pass the time, and to keep my mind off darker thoughts, I took 'Myths and Folklore' from my bag and laid it on my lap. I had often heard about the legendary Hairy-Backed Forest Hog and wished to know more. I discovered that the hog has a particularly interesting diet, which fact I noted in view of my vengeful intent. Indeed I grew quite excited to think how my plan was starting to take shape. At that moment, however, a tremendous clap of thunder interrupted my reading and the ground shook with the ferocity of the clashing heavens. So involved was I in my book and plotting I had failed to notice the returning storm. Searing bolts of lightning lit up the sky. The repairs, and the courage of the horses, were tested to their limits as with every gust of wind the carriage rocked violently on its springs. I had to brace myself not to be flung through the door.

I dared to look out only once, to see that we

were climbing, merely feet away from the edge of a precipitous drop. In the brief moments between the thunder and lightning I could hear Solomon swearing at the horses and the sound of his whip. I huddled on the seat with my cloak wrapped around me and began to pray fervently for safe delivery to Withypitts Hall. Just when I thought that fear had brought me as close to death as it was possible to be while still breathing, the carriage came to an unsteady halt.

Solomon's face appeared at the hatch in the roof. He was red-cheeked and wet. 'I can go no further,' he shouted above the wind. 'You'll have to continue on foot.'

I pulled my hat down so hard on my head that it pinched my ears. With the parcel of books under one arm and my bag over my shoulder I opened the door, fighting to hold it in the wind, and jumped down to sink ankle deep in freezing soupy mud. I could feel the chill water seeping through the seams of my boots. Grimacing and cursing I made my way to firmer ground and looked ahead.

At first I saw nothing. The moon was behind the swollen clouds and the sheeting rain made everything blurry. But then pitchforked lightning split the inky sky and my heart faltered. In its white light my disbelieving eyes saw a vast jagged silhouette stretching across a broad mountainous outcrop like a diabolical gathering of crouching devils. Their horns were the towers and the lights burning in the windows their evil red eyes.

'Tartri flammis!' I breathed, and could say not another word. This behemoth before me was Withypitts Hall.

'This is madness!' shouted Solomon. 'Come back with me. It's not too late.'

I tried to answer but my words were blown back in my face so I just shook my head. Solomon shrugged in helpless disbelief. He clapped me on the shoulder, wished me luck and hauled himself back on to his seat. I stared again at the looming Hall and when I looked back the carriage had already turned and was gathering speed down the hill. Now my only choice was to go on.

I pushed on up the road, tripping and sliding and skidding, and within minutes I was soaked through. I must have battled against the storm for nigh on half an hour before finally reaching the huge iron gates that flanked the broad gravelled carriageway up to the main doors. Intermittent lightning flashes allowed me to see for only seconds at a time the full extent of the building: the six tall towers that reached up to the black clouds, the tall, narrow leaded windows, atop the arched pinnacles of which sat grinning devils and the roof edge supported by gargoyles of the most repulsive nature.

Close now to exhaustion I staggered up the steps. In the centre of the oaken door was a huge brass knocker in the shape of a hog's head. It took all my remaining strength to lift it with both hands and bring it down upon the ancient wood. The impact resounded within and was immediately answered by a cacophony of howling dogs. Then as I waited I thought I heard a different sound, neither animal nor human but the strains of a tune, a high-pitched and mournful air that was soon swallowed by the wind.

With a ghastly groaning the door finally opened. A skeletal man towered over me and took in my bedraggled state with dull, unforgiving eyes. His etiolated pallor was like a plant that had never seen the sun.

'Yes?' he said. He elongated the single syllable in a low monotone.

'I have a delivery,' I croaked. 'For Lady Mandible.'

'What is it, Gerulphus?' enquired a second, higher pitched voice. A lady came up behind him, in a voluminous skirt, with the darkest hair you have ever seen and wide shining eyes of violet hue and full blood-red lips.

'It's a boy, Your Ladyship,' replied Gerulphus slowly. 'Just a boy.'

I tried to speak but again, from somewhere within the Hall, I heard the music. It rose to a merciless crescendo, filling my ears and ringing in my head until I could hardly think.

And that is the last thing I remember. Exhaustion overcame me and in an instant everything went dark and I fell an indeterminate distance to the ground.

Chapter Fifteen

Arrival

After his collapse on the steps of Withypitts Hall, Hector awoke in a far better place. He came to on a couch of the softest velvet in a chamber of flickering lights. From the domed ceiling above him hung a many-tiered chandelier with a hundred or more glittering candles.

Slowly he looked around and was so taken with the gilded furniture, the oriental patterned flocked wallpaper, the sumptuous dark curtains, the black marble fireplace in which roared a gloriously red and orange fire, that it was some moments before he became aware of the other people in the room.

'He is awake, My Lady,' said the unmistakable voice of

Gerulphus. He was standing directly behind the couch.

Hector's bemused gaze met the curious stare of the lady with the sanguine-hued lips. She was sitting opposite on a cream silken chaise longue and cooling herself languorously with a peacock-feather fan. Closing the fan with a snap she beckoned him over.

'Come closer,' she said. Her voice was soft yet commanding. If it was a colour, Hector thought, it would be deep brown. 'Have a seat.' There was a small stool beside her chaise longue and in front of it a low table set with a platter of colourful sweets. Beside that stood a tall silver spouted pot, a delicately patterned cup with matching sugar bowl, and a crystal glass and jug filled to the brim with sparkling amber liquid. Hector stood up and his feet sank into the thick grey wolfskin rug (complete with head, fangs and yellow eyes) that lay between the two couches.

He sat carefully on the edge of the stool, acutely aware of the state of his clothes. He was also aware of how ravenously hungry he was and couldn't help but stare longingly at the dainty aromatic treats that teased his nose. They smelled of marzipan and dark chocolate and were decorated with bright red cherries and raisins and iced in swirls.

'Do you know who I am?'

'You are Lady Mandible,' said Hector slowly, 'and this is Withypitts Hall.'

'And what is your name?'

'Hector. The Baron sent a carriage for me.'

'Ah, the butterfly boy,' rejoined Lady Mandible. 'I thought as much. You are very welcome.' She looked at him closely. 'Are you hungry?'

Hector had always been told it was not polite to openly admit to hunger, but after his sojourn in Fitch's Home his manners were not as they once were. Hardly able to take his eyes off the platter, he nodded vigorously.

'Then take one.'

She pointed to the sweets and he noticed for the first time that her painted nails were neither rounded nor squared off, but sharpened almost to talons. She wore a large ring on every finger, each with a gleaming oversized dark stone.

'Take as many as you like. I have them brought in specially. No one around here has the skills to make such delicate treats.' She laughed, rather cruelly. 'And very few people deserve them.'

Hector needed no more encouragement. He dropped a sweet into his mouth and was caught by surprise at the intensity of the taste, the sensation of the chocolate slowly melting, its sweetness running down the back of his throat. Before he could help himself he had eaten another and taken two more. He was ready to cram them in as well but a sudden shiver ran down his spine and he managed to stop himself. Lady Mandible's unblinking eyes were fixed upon him, her head slightly cocked, and she was opening and closing her fan.

Gerulphus approached noiselessly, as seemed to be his way. He was like a creature that had once been alive, Hector thought, then had died and been brought back from the grave. He filled for Hector a glass from the jug of sweet ginger beer. Then he lifted and tipped the silver pot. A stream of dark liquid ran from its spout into the patterned cup. Hector looked at the manservant's bony wrists protruding from his cuffs and could see pulsing blue veins running up the back of his hands. The bittersweet aroma of the liquid was very familiar to Hector. One of the most expensive coffees you could buy, his father used to serve it when entertaining important wine merchants. This, mingled with the taste and smell of the treats, the ginger beer and the heady perfume that wafted from his hostess, combined to make him feel a little light-headed.

Lady Mandible looked at him quizzically and reached across to take a marzipan delicacy for herself at the same time as Hector. Her fingers brushed over his hand and he flinched. Her nails were sharp as blades and her skin abnormally cool.

'I believe you brought something for me too,' she said.

Gerulphus handed her Perigoe's parcel and a knife and she cut the string with a slashing motion then placed the package on the table and flattened down the oilskin to reveal a pile of books. She lifted the top one, a large brown-covered volume, and it fell open to show a full-page colour plate of a butterfly. Hector's heart ached at the sight of the beautiful creature. It was a painful reminder of his previous life but also of his purpose. If he really wanted revenge on the Baron, he had to win this job.

'*Argynnis paphia*,' he said quickly. 'A Silver-Washed Fritillary.'

'So, the Baron was right,' remarked Lady Mandible. 'But what a puzzle you are. A knowledge of Latin and butterflies, and yet by all appearances you are an urchin.'

'My father bred and collected them,' explained Hector under her cool gaze.

'Where are your parents?'

116

'Dead. Both of them.'

'Lord Mandible lost his father last year,' she said vaguely. 'Poor Burleigh, he was most upset.' She sipped at her coffee and shrugged. 'Now, about the butterflies. As you know, the Mandible Midwinter Feast is unrivalled for miles –' she looked at Hector and he nodded quickly in agreement – 'and this year I am going to make sure it stays that way forever. For that I need butterflies, hundreds of them, but they must all be big and colourful, no dull browns or bland whites.'

Hector thought for a moment. 'I know one that would be perfect for a display,' he said. 'Is that what you have in mind?'

'A display? I suppose you could call it that.'

'I am thinking of *Papilio ingenspennatus*,' he continued, picturing the colourful butterfly his father had shown him that last night before everything changed. 'An enormous butterfly, with spectacular multicoloured wings the size of your hands. No two are alike.'

Lady Mandible leaned forward and her eyes sparkled. 'Can you get them for the very day I need them?'

'For the very hour,' said Hector, somewhat recklessly. 'I can control the hatching through temperature.'

'Well, well,' she said finally, with a look that seemed to penetrate his skull. 'If you *can* do all you say, then you must stay here at the Hall and provide the butterflies for the Feast. But be sure that you can. I don't like people who break promises.'

'I always keep my word,' said Hector firmly, 'but I will need money, to buy the cocoons and equipment. There is a supplier in Urbs Umida –'

Lady Mandible raised her hand dismissively. 'You can have anything you want. Ask Gerulphus. Just make sure the butterflies are ready on the night.' Her smile was engaging but there was a hint of menace in her voice and Hector remembered Perigoe's warning.

Sensing that the conversation was drawing to a close, Hector stood up but before he could take a step the door opened and a man entered the room. All eyes turned in his direction. Lady Mandible arched an eyebrow in greeting as Hector's heart fluttered.

The man was Baron Bovrik de Vandolin.

Bovrik's eye sought only Lady Mandible and he came straight over to kiss her outstretched hand. Hector, slowly recovering from the bilious feeling that rose in his gullet upon seeing the Baron again, took the opportunity to look at him properly. His clothes could only be described as riotous in their colour, and he wore an eyepatch that matched his cravat perfectly. As before, the faint smell of citrus lingered in the air around him.

'Ah, Bovrik,' said Lady Mandible with a clap of delight. 'This is Hector, found half dead with exhaustion on the steps – the boy from the City you told me about. I must commend you, sir. He is quite a find.'

Bovrik sat on a nearby chair and absentmindedly stroked the furry cushions, as if they were an animal of some sort. He looked at Hector with his one eye and an odd smile.

'I am glad that he meets your high expectations,' he said. Then, with an exaggerated flourish, he turned to Lady Mandible and pulled off the eyepatch.

'Oh, Bovrik, not another one!' she sighed with seemingly mock ennui, drumming her glittering fingers on the ivory handle of her fan. 'Are you expecting to lose your right eye as well? At least you will have enough eyeballs to fill both sockets! What jewel is it this time?'

Bovrik deliberately faced Hector, who could now see clearly the white scar that ran through the Baron's eyebrow to finish under his eye. In the socket was the false eyeball Lady Mandible spoke of, with a pale blue iris to match his good eye. It was sparkling in the light and Hector suddenly realized there was a jewel set into the black pupil. The effect was quite odd and unnerving: it was difficult enough to be so close to a man when you knew his fate was in your hands without this ludicrous display.

'An emerald, Lady Mandible,' said Bovrik, without looking away from Hector. It was as if, Hector thought, he sensed his discomfort. Suddenly the villain jerked his head sharply forward and then back up and Hector let out a small involuntary shout, for Bovrik's socket was now black and empty, the eyeball instead staring blankly up at him from the Baron's palm.

Lady Mandible giggled archly. 'Hector, you look positively distressed,' she said. ''Tis only an eye. I thought you were made of sterner stuff.'

'You will need to be,' said Bovrik dryly as he pushed the eyeball back in.

'Now, Bovrik,' said Lady Mandible officiously, turning back to the Baron. 'Tell me how it goes with preparations for the Feast while Gerulphus shows the boy to his room.'

'Indeed.' Bovrik flicked a finger in the manservant's direction. 'You heard your mistress – get to it! Leef us finer folk to our culinary con-fer-sa-tion.'

Gerulphus's expression did not change as he regarded the Baron for a moment. Then he bowed, tapped Hector on the shoulder and left the room. It was with great relief that Hector followed him.

Chapter Sixteen

A Letter to Polly

Dear Polly,

I have been at Withypitts Hall almost ten days now
and I am much better acquainted with things. After my
first encounter with Lady Mandible (and He-Who-Shall-
Not-Be-Named), Gerulphus led me back through the
entrance hall (I had my wits about me this time) and I
saw that the walls were adorned with hunting trophies
from previous generations: stags, bears, mountain lions,
dozens of pairs of antlers of varying sizes and points,
even a Jocastar - such a rare and unusual creature, I

thought its large eyes and delicate features out of place with the other animals. But these were all outdone by a huge and savage-looking hog's head - that of a Hairy-Back, of course - which takes pride of place in the middle of the display. It was caught by the old Lord Mandible. His son hunts the hog almost daily, but with less success. I have seen neither the beast's head of which Oscar spoke nor the chair, and I can't say I'm upset to have missed them. It would not surprise me if that villain has them in his own private rooms - that would fit his twisted nature.

Gerulphus led me to what I judged to be the furthest corner of the Hall, the west wing, to one of the towers. We climbed a steep stone staircase, sharply winding, and I suspected none had ventured up it for many years. Cobwebs as thick as table lace tangled in my hair and bats flew about my head. The smell caused me to choke. As for the room at the top, my room, it is spacious but on my arrival it contained just a bed, a chair and a table. During the week I have acquired the luxury of a chamber pot and water jug. And I am comfortable enough. There is a fireplace and I have managed to light a fire, though the chimney smokes quite badly.

In many ways Withypitts is a most beautiful residence. The floors are laid with intricate mosaics, the walls adorned with all manner of tapestries and pictures, statues and carvings are everywhere and all glitters as gold. But the longer I am here, the more I begin to see that Lady Mandible's ubiquitous touch is always apparent and somehow the beauty is spoilt. Her taste for extravagance might not extend to the servants' quarters but perhaps I should be grateful that neither does her taste for the queer. This is why the Pagus Parvus villagers warned me about her.

Withypitts Hall is not a warm place in any sense of the word. Take, as an example, the ceiling in the great dining hall (where the Feast is to be held). It is painted with nebulous scenes from the heavens but if you look more closely you see that behind the angels mischievous little sprites thumb their noses and adopt rude poses. On pedestals up and down the corridors stuffed animals pose stiffly, fear in their glassy eyes, snarling and frozen in time. Foxes, weasels, squirrels - every creature of the forest is represented. But these are hardly the worst of it. There are many other objects on display that would be better placed in an exhibition of oddities. Lady Mandible has a liking for the more gruesome collectables: saints' bones, death masks and thumb-prickers. And in the darker recesses she keeps freakish unborn animal specimens suspended in liquid in glass jars, claiming a scientific interest. To walk past these things is even worse at night. Which brings me to the point of my letter.

The morning after my arrival, Gerulphus showed me to a small, north-facing room on the third floor where I am to breed the butterflies. I refer to it as the Hatchery or 'Incunabulorum'. It is dark and very cool, as per my specifications, and Gerulphus has since procured for me all that I require from the City. I spent a day setting up the tanks for my cocoons. I will keep them in a state of suspended animation until the time is right and then I will warm them up so they can emerge in their ultimate manifestation. It is not an exact process, of course, but I think I am capable of producing what Lady Mandible wishes. Her final purpose is still unknown to me but in many respects I am equivocal about it. The butterflies will not survive long afterwards anyway - once hatched they live no more than a few days in the wild. Besides, my mind, as you know, is on other matters.

And, dear Polly, it was these very matters that kept me awake the other night. Then, as I brooded over my butterfly tanks, I heard a noise outside the room and when I looked out I saw the very person I had just been thinking of creeping round the corner at the end of the hall and out of sight. The so-called Baron! My curiosity aroused I set off after him. But by the time I reached the next corner he had already disappeared and I had to give up the chase.

As I returned to the Incunabulorum I thought hard about what I had just witnessed. It was hardly out of character for Bovrik to have some new trick up his sleeve, but what did this signify? I resolved to keep a much closer eye on him in future - I can't let his plans get in the way of my carrying out my own. I have proved myself capable of solving almost any riddle thrown at me, as will I now. I will not let him outwit me again.

In the day it is easier to keep an eye on Bovrik. He visits me almost daily to check on my progress. Every moment in his presence is akin to suffering, especially as he is so high and mighty, always acting his part and turning the strange glint of his latest glass eye upon me whenever possible, but I grit my teeth and answer his questions and wait for him to go. At least my plan begins to take even firmer shape. The night of the Feast - I don't think it can be done before then - will be remembered, and not just for Lady Mandible's butterflies. I cannot say more than that, for fear of discovery.

When not in my Incunabulorum I spend much of my time in the Hall kitchen. Mrs Malherbe, the cook, a lady of similar girth to height, has been most welcoming. She complains daily about all the preparations for the Feast. Lady Mandible wishes it to be based on Trimalchio's Feast. I recall his tale from my studies of the Classics with my tutor. Trimalchio was a character in a Roman story by Petronius. Once a slave, he gained his freedom and attained great wealth and power. He was renowned thereafter for his ostentatious and lavish banquets. When I told Mrs Malherbe this she merely grunted.

The other servants like to talk about the City. They are aware of its cruel and violent nature and I have not disabused them. I told them of my riddling, and now they beseech me daily for entertainment. This

127

morning I gave them the riddle of the evil queen (I will write it at the end for your amusement).

Naturally, the conversation often turns to the Mandibles themselves. Lord Mandible apparently is a very different fish to his wife. I have seen him but once or twice. He is not much to look at. His head is brachycephalic in shape, being much wider than it is long, and he is balding even though he is still at a young age. When he walks he drags his withered leg and his breeches rustle, making it quite impossible for him to sneak up on a person, unlike Gerulphus who appears and disappears like a silent ghost. Lord Mandible has two interests, hog hunting and his father's harpsichord. If not at one, he is at the other. My ears have not quite attuned to his style of playing. He keeps a pair of cats by the names of Posset and Percy, of which he is very fond. Occasionally one or the other walks across the harpsichord keys and, in truth, it is difficult to tell which of the three might be playing.

But Lady Mandible does not suffer in her husband's absence for if Gerulphus is not at her side, then Bovrik is. A sort of human parasite hanging on her every word, Bovrik likes to give his opinion too. She appears to listen but it is difficult to tell what is going through her mind. I have seen that look before - it is common among those on the north side of the river. She strikes me as a fickle sort, in need of constant amusement and easily bored. In the past week alone she has ordered that all the drapes must be changed. Mrs Malherbe says, with some contempt, that they have been hung no more than six months. It is no secret in the kitchen that Mrs Malherbe prefers Lord Mandible (he likes her pies) and she has no time for his wife's extravagances. As for the Baron, there's no love lost there either. She thinks him a prancing, posing, untrustworthy sort of fellow and she is quite convinced he communes with the Devil on a regular basis. Besides, she says, she couldn't trust a man who won't look you straight in the eye, regardless of the fact he only has one. As you can imagine, I have not disagreed with her on this.

As I learned so painfully upon my arrival, Withypitts Hall is set atop a rocky outcrop in the mountains. It has been snowing most days since I arrived and all too often we are enveloped in thick grey fog. On the odd occasion the sky has cleared I have looked out of my four windows. The surrounding gardens are pleasantly titivated, with plenty of winter foliage, and stretch in every direction until they reach the boundary wall, ten feet tall and built from mountain rock. In the distance you can see the highest snow-capped peaks even deeper into the Moiraean Mountains range. To the east is the ancient oak forest, the home of the legendary Hairy-Backed Hog. It was often served for supper when Father was alive.

And so time is passing. The Feast draws nearer. I travelled from the west to reach the Hall, and on the days I can see the road that leads back to Pagus Parvus and on to the City. I think of you, Polly, and hope one day to see you again.

Salve,
Your friend,
Hector

P.S. The Riddle of the Evil Queen - as promised

There was once a wicked queen who lived in a wonderful palace in the mountains. She decided one day to build another palace so she sent her guards to the villages and told them to bring back all the young men to build it. Of course the young men didn't want to leave their homes, and one demanded to speak to the queen, to complain about how unfairly she was treating them all. Impressed by his spirit the queen decided to give him a chance.

'Come with me,' she said, and he followed her out to the castle gardens.

She held up a small bag. 'Into this bag my servant will put two stones, a black one and a white one. You will draw from the bag one stone. If it is black you will work for me, if it is white you will go home.'

The young man agreed, but not fully trusting the queen he watched the servant closely. To his horror his keen eyes saw the servant place two black stones in the bag.

'Draw,' commanded the queen.

What did the young man do?

If you cannot solve it, Polly, I promise to tell you the answer when next I see you!

Chapter Seventeen

A Toast

Baron Bovrik de Vandolin laid down a recent copy of the *Diurnal Journal* on the bedside pot locker (a necessary evil in the tower rooms, the newly installed water closet being some distance away) and cast an eye over his breakfast tray, a sumptuous feast of coddled goose eggs and slices of Hairy-Back ham – such a delicacy! Its meat was addictive, more succulent, more aromatic, more satisfying than any other. Once you had tasted a Hairy's ham no other swine's could ever match it. And for Bovrik the taste was always bittersweet. He loved and hated the Hairy-Backed Hog because with every delicious mouthful he was reminded of where he had ended up and of his own true and lowly beginnings . . .

'Those days are long gone,' he thought with a shudder of relief as he mopped up the juices with a slice of bread. His eye flicked back to the sketch on the open page of the journal. Yes, it did him justice, and Lady Mandible too.

Looking around himself Bovrik still couldn't believe just how well things had turned out. He resided in the highest, most spacious tower of the six at Withypitts Hall, lavishly and gaudily furnished exactly as he would have done it himself. The sumptuousness of the surroundings seemed to physically thicken the air. His bed, a large four-poster, was specially shaped to fit against the curved wall and he sat under a gold-embroidered velvet cover which fell to the floor, where its fringed hem sat in soft undulations. He was surrounded by plump orange pillows and he leaned against a tasselled short-furred bolster that stretched across the full width of the bed. The curtains were also of velvet, scarlet with thick coiled golden ties, like ships' ropes, and golden fringes. The wooden floor – those parts which were exposed – shone almost like a mirror as a result of hours of polishing. The remainder was covered in soft-furred bearskin rugs. Sometimes Bovrik just threw himself on the fur and rolled around in its deep, enveloping loveliness. Other times he would sit in his feather-cushioned armchair, wrap himself up in his cloak and rub its expensive Jocastar fringe all over his face.

All this, of course, was done with the door locked.

Since his latest metamorphosis his life had changed immeasurably for the better and he congratulated himself daily on the success of his latest swindle. His plan had been simple enough: in the guise of an exotic foreigner (north Urbs Umidians loved the exotic) to charm his way into the wealthy circles of the City and live the rich life he had so long envied. He would find ways to relieve those around him of their valuables, large and small (to be disposed of by Badlesmire and Leavelund via their contacts in the Nimble Finger), to keep him in pocket. Perhaps trick an old, wealthy lady or two into writing him into their will, maybe even marry one . . .

And what a great start it had been. With his new wardrobe, mysterious accent and bottomless reservoir of charm, not to mention his ever-expanding collection of eyeballs, he had been welcomed with open arms into northside society. After all, as Hector himself well knew, the north side was a place where people were judged in the main on appearance. The ladies in particular had taken to him and he was invited into all the best drawing rooms. He might have arrived with only his personality but he always left with a memento — a ring, an ornament, a piece of cutlery, all items small enough that they wouldn't be missed for a while. Indeed sometimes, if he had been shaken, he would have jangled like Christmas bells.

But it was his encounter with Lady Mandible that set him on a fateful and even more lucrative course.

Lady Lysandra Mandible was well known in Urbs Umida. Her wealth — rightly rumoured to be significant — had been rapidly attained by a succession of marriages to rich, much older men. She came to the City just when old Lord Mandible, painfully aware of young Lord Mandible's shortcomings, was seeking a wife for him to ensure the continuation of the family line. Lysandra suited both Mandibles' purposes eminently, and vice versa, and they were married while Bovrik, as Gulliver Truepin, was still selling hair restorer elsewhere.

It was at the Annual Northside Late Summer Ball that Bovrik was introduced to Lady Lysandra. She, having heard much about this charming and popular foreigner, thought it would be both practical and amusing to engage him to help with the Midwinter Feast. And of course she knew how it would gall so many society ladies if she was to have the delectable Baron all to herself. Bovrik, for completely different reasons, was equally happy to accept the position and lost no time installing himself at Withypitts Hall.

'Ah,' murmured Bovrik, running his hand over the crisp linen sheet. 'This is living!' This was certainly the most enjoyable and profitable swindle he had ever undertaken. He had already recouped all the money he'd spent to get here by pilfering Mandible trinkets, and he was able to do it in such style and comfort. Even if he only stayed at Withypitts until the Feast, he was sure to have significantly increased his wealth.

With a self-satisfied smile he took an engraved rectangular box from beside the bed and opened it to reveal a red velvet-lined interior with seven deep depressions, four of which were occupied with false eyeballs. There they sat, side by side, all staring the same way. At first glance they looked identical – made from glass, off-white with a jet-black pupil and a pale blue iris. Upon closer inspection, however, it could be seen that each had a jewel or precious stone in the centre of the pupil, winking in the light, and that each jewel was different: a ruby, an opal, a pearl and the most recent emerald.

'Hmm,' he thought, snapping the box shut. 'Three to go,

and then I will have one for every day of the week.'

He sighed deeply. Regardless of his heart's desire, he had decided that when he had his final eyeball – by the Feast, he hoped – he would leave. Years of swindling had taught him never to push his luck in one place too long. It was a rule he prided himself on. He screwed up his face. But it pained him to think of walking away from such a wonderful meal ticket and, against his better judgement, recently he had found himself wondering if he could postpone his departure. Lady Mandible, in some ways such a kindred spirit, certainly seemed to enjoy his company. She liked his suggestions for the Feast (it was he who had first mentioned Trimalchio), and with the somewhat unseemly connections he had made over the years he was able to help her with some of her more 'unusual' ideas about decor and entertainment. She was obviously delighted with the so-called butterfly boy too. That had been a stroke of luck. Until his encounter with Hector Bovrik had been rather stumped as to where to find hundreds of butterflies in winter.

'Oh, surely there is a way . . .' he mused. He stroked his cloak thoughtfully again. The fur seemed to represent everything that was important to him.

'And why should Jocastar not be for the likes of me?' he

thought with some bitterness. 'I'm worth it.'

He looked out across the grounds and down the hill to the ancient oak forest and he remembered once again a day long ago when he was still young Jereome Hogsherd, son of Tucker Hogsherd, a lowly forest dweller . . .

Chapter Eighteen

Thanks for the Memory

. . . That autumn morning, young Jereome sat by the stream watching his father's pigs (he always referred to them as his father's, distancing himself from their ownership) rooting about and chewing on acorns. He was deep in thought as usual, lamenting his life of drudgery and pig filth, and it was some time before he realized that he was no longer alone. A solitary traveller, a rangy man with a narrow head and high cheekbones, had managed to come unnoticed up to the stream and stood quite close to him. Jereome said nothing. He had little interest in strangers, especially ones who looked impoverished. If the fellow had money (and Jereome had a unique ability to sniff it out), it would have been a different story. Certainly he would have introduced himself in the hope of taking advantage of the stranger's purse. In fact, if Jereome had known just a little more about the stranger, his life could have taken a very different course, but that is by the by.

Eventually Jereome sneaked a better look at the fellow only to find that he was already under close scrutiny himself. The traveller looked as if he had been on the road for some time. He carried a knapsack and a stick and was plainly dressed, in dark colours. With a curt nod to Jereome he knelt by the stream and took a drink of water from cupped hands.

Jereome was wary of strangers. Generally they meant trouble. Either they wanted hospitality (for which the forest dwellers were not known at all, having a reputation to the contrary) or they were sheriffs looking for criminals. This man didn't look like a sheriff. He watched as the man laid down his bag and took out a hunk of bread, some cheese and a bottle of ale.

'Would you like to share with me?' he asked. His accent was not local but also not strong enough to place anywhere else.

'I have my own,' said Jereome, and pulled from his pocket

some strips of dark dried meat. And to his surprise, almost without realizing he was doing it, he offered a piece to the stranger. The man's eyes lit up and he took it gratefully.

'Hairy-Backed Hog,' he said as he chewed it. 'Excellent! The best there is.'

Jereome's chest puffed out. 'I cured it myself,' he said.

'And what a fine job you've done. Here, take some bread, make a meal of it.'

Jereome accepted and the two sat silently for some minutes chewing and drinking, the stranger from his ale bottle and Bovrik from his water-filled pig's bladder.

Finally replete, the two began a conversation in earnest. Nearby the pigs were snuffling and the trees were swaying gently in the breeze. The weak sun had mustered some strength and they both enjoyed the feel of its rays on their faces.

'So, where have you come from?' asked Jereome. 'Where do you go?'

'I have come from a small town in the midlands.' The man mentioned a name that was familiar to Jereome. 'Perhaps you have heard of it?'

'And what were you doing there?'

The stranger laughed. 'What I always do. Trying to help but getting into trouble.'

'You sound as if it wasn't quite what you expected.'

'Oh, I expected it all right,' said the man. 'Some things are inevitable.'

Jereome was quietly intrigued by this enigmatic stranger. 'Tell me more,' he urged. 'Have you had any adventure? What was your reward?'

'Adventure? Certainly. Reward? Well, I have this,' said the man and he produced from his rucksack a wooden leg.

Jereome glanced immediately and overtly at the man's legs. He recalled that he had limped as he had approached.

'I limp, it is true,' said the stranger, seeing his look, 'but I do have both my legs. This wooden leg belonged to a very old gentleman. I had the privilege of hearing his last confession on his deathbed. He gave it to me before he passed on.'

'What would anyone want with a wooden leg? Is it valuable?'

'Not the leg itself,' replied the man, 'but what was in it. Look.'

He held it out and twisted the knee and it came off. The leg was hollow. 'The man kept his life savings in it, in promissory letters and bank notes. It was a substantial sum.'

'What of the man's family?'

'Aha! Now you get to the crux of it. The gentleman did

have a son but he was a slothful beast. He knew what was in the leg and he came to me and demanded that I give it to him, that it was his by right. I refused, of course. He threatened me and then left. He returned that evening and stole it when he thought I wasn't looking.'

'Were you? Looking, I mean?'

'I'll grant you that I was not surprised when he came back.'

'What about the money?'

The traveller laughed. 'Let's just say when he put his hand in the leg he got a nasty surprise.'

Jereome frowned. 'When he found there was no money?'

'Yes, that too.'

Now Jereome was confused. 'If not money, then what *did* he find?' he asked.

The stranger got to his feet and, with some difficulty, pushed the leg into his knapsack again. He smiled oddly.

'Just a little something that had crawled in unexpectedly – and completely of its own accord, I hasten to add.'

'Like a scorpion, perhaps?'

'Similar. Certainly the encounter was fatal.'

'But you have the leg still.'

143

'I like to think it came back to its rightful owner.'

'So why do you keep it?'

'I have a feeling that it will come in useful one day.' The stranger stretched and yawned. 'Well,' he said with finality, 'I must be on my way. I have a long journey. I am heading further into the mountains.'

Jereome shuddered. 'Why do you want to go there? It will be so cold this time of year and only get colder. You should stay in the forest. Wait out the winter.'

'No, I must go,' said the stranger. 'I am . . .' he hesitated before finishing softly, '. . . expected.' He looked at Jereome with a critical eye until the boy began to feel as if he was being measured up for something. But then the man gave a little shake of his head and began to gather his things.

'I wish you well,' said Jereome uncharacteristically, and shook his hand. 'Maybe one day we will meet again.'

'Perhaps,' said the stranger, and put his cloak around his shoulders. As it swung about him it brushed against Jereome's bare skin. The hairs stood up on his arm and his body tingled all over. Such softness! He had never felt such a thing. Jereome's clothes were woven by his own mother and were coarse and stiff and smelled quite bad when they were wet, which at this time of year was most days. Almost shocked by the feel of the cloak, Jereome watched as the tall stranger began to walk away.

'Wait,' he called after him. 'I have a question.'

The man had already stopped.

'Your cloak. From what material is it made?'

'Jocastar,' said the man, 'naturally.' And then he disappeared into the forest, leaving Jereome in a frenzy of emotions. He realized he had never even asked the stranger his name.

And what of the money in the leg? thought Jereome, but by now it was too late.

That night over bacon stew and acorn broth Jereome spoke to his family about the stranger.

'Jocastar?' queried his father with a frown. 'Don't you be getting any ideas about that,' he said gruffly. 'Jocastar ain't for the likes of us. The most expensive fur in the world, woven into the finest material. The creature is found only on the highest slopes of the mountains. Fools alone go to harvest it. There certainly ain't none around here.'

'I . . . .' began Jereome, but his father's expression did not invite any more conversation.

That night Jereome lay awake until the early hours, his mind in turmoil. The feel of the cloak still made his finger-tips tingle. Suddenly, Jocastar seemed to represent everything that he wanted, and yet was denied, from life. Jereome did not subscribe to the same self-perpetuating martyrdom as his father. He had plans for his future suddenly and it didn't involve the forest. Or pigs.

'Why should that traveller, a man of little fortune by all appearances, have such a luxurious item and I not?' he asked himself. 'Is he any better than I am?'

And he vowed that night to one day possess a cloak of Jocastar and all the things that went with it . . .

Bovrik shook himself from his reverie. The irony of his situation – that he was living such a high life only a few miles from where he was born a lowly peasant – never failed to make him smile.

He sprayed some of his favourite lemon perfume into the air, walked quickly through the aromatic cloud and then turned back to his box of eyeballs, to select one for the day.

'Eeenie meenie minie mo
How I wish Lord M would go
Bovrik then could rule the show
Eenie meenie minie mo.'

146

His glass eye successfully chosen, he lifted his cup, filled with tea brewed from tea leaves picked by finger and thumb at elbow height from the rarest of tea bushes that grew only in secret locations in the Orient, Lady Mandible's favourite, and toasted the air.

'To you, Augustus Fitzbaudly,' he said. 'I couldn't have done it without you.' Now, where was that boy? He had an errand for him to run. He did so like having servants to order around.

Chapter Nineteen

A Close Encounter

Hector was trying his utmost to breathe quietly but he was tense and his chest was tight. He was crouched down awkwardly in a bush and a branch was poking him in the back of the head, but he couldn't afford to make a sound. In front of him was a small clearing in what was otherwise the dark and dense forest of centuries-old oak, the source of so much of the Hall's interior – the panelling on the walls, the broad floorboards (where it was not marble) and, of course, the huge dining table in the main dining hall.

It was sleeting but Hector was well wrapped up in his father's cloak. He had the hood pulled right over his head and the green cloth allowed him to melt into his surroundings.

No one could possibly have known that he was there. No *one*, that is, but not no *thing*.

A Hairy-Backed Forest Hog stood only feet away from his hiding place.

The hog, a magnificent and certainly most hairy specimen, was the largest member of the pig family Hector had ever seen. It looked ancient, its whiskers were grey, but the ridge along its back was just as he had heard, jet black, with all the appearance of scorched fur. There had been rumours for some time in the Hall, greeted with great excitement by Lord Mandible, about a couple of extra-large hogs roaming the forest but sightings were few and far between. There was no doubt in Hector's mind, however, that this was one of those very creatures.

This was the third time Hector had ventured into the forest in as many days. The Baron had sent word again that Lady Mandible needed a large quantity of hog hair and Hector had accepted the task. He was happy to run errands – as long as the cocoons stayed cool they needed little attention, and he found it suited his mood better to keep busy. Besides, it was in his own interest to visit the forest . . . The Hairy-Back was a copious shedder regardless of the time of year, so the bristle was readily found on the forest floor and caught in bushes and briars. It had many uses at the Hall, from false eyelashes to cushion stuffing to cosmetic brushes. He had gathered a full bag on the two previous occasions without incident but today things were not going so smoothly.

The hog lifted its long fleshy snout into the air and sniffed audibly. It seemed to Hector the beast knew he was there. Its head was cocked slightly to one side as it stared unblinking into the foliage. Two huge yellowing canines rose from its lower jaw, glistening with toxic saliva, to fit perfectly side by side with the pair that grew down from the upper.

'It must weigh as much as my horse,' he thought.

The hog sniffed again and then began to root about in the forest floor. Finding what it was looking for, it started to eat noisily, its jaw grinding from side to side. Then with a satisfied snort it turned and trotted back into the trees. Hector allowed himself to breathe again. It was a privilege to have seen the animal but it was also a relief to see it go. Many a huntsman, generally dead, bore the scars of those canines.

As he crawled out from the bush he noticed something glinting on the ground in front of him. He picked it up. It was a huge ring, heavy and cold in his hand. Its black stone gleamed even in the forest's low light. How had that got there? he wondered. Still, he was fortunate. If the ring was as valuable as it felt, it would fetch him good money when he sold it. Hector was very aware that when his plan was complete a rapid exit from the Hall might be necessary, and any extra funds he had to help him on his way would be most useful. He put it in his pocket.

Standing up, Hector went to where the hog had been rooting. He could clearly see the remains of its mushroom meal. The hog ate only the large juicy heads, leaving the long narrow stalks in the ground, which stalks were exactly what Hector was after.

Once finished, Hector pulled off his gloves and tucked them inside out into his pocket, alongside the ring. Then he unpicked a large tuft of hog hair from a nearby branch, stuffed it into the overfull pouch at his hip, and started back through the forest. He had left his mare tethered to a branch when the trees grew too close for her to get through.

He hadn't gone far when he stopped in his tracks and pricked up his ears. The thickness of the undergrowth meant it was difficult to see but he could hear. And what he heard was the unmistakable sound of a snorting, bellowing, charging hog. He didn't even turn to look before breaking into a wild and desperate run. As he crashed through the undergrowth and the low hanging branches he cursed inwardly. He should have known. These forest hogs were not only renowned for their hirsute nature and their supremely tasty flesh, but also for their short temper and cunning. Of course it was going to come after him; it was just biding its time. He should have kept watch over his shoulder but there were so many other things on his mind nowadays that he was not as alert as usual.

Although the Hairy-Backed Forest Hog is abnormally big for a woodland pig, owing much of his bulk to pure fat (which is why he is so exceedingly tasty), this is no hindrance at all to his speed and agility. To see a Hairy-Back in full flight, his head down, his eyes fixed and staring, his trotters tearing up the mud, is a sight and a half. Imagine it: those bristled, fatty flanks swaying from side to side, the dark flesh rippling from back to front and back again in rhythm with his gallop. The sight alone is breathtaking in the extreme . . . but the noise! His roaring grunt is more akin to that of a lion than a swine. Crashing through the undergrowth he comes, his charge gathering momentum, allowing nothing in his path to divert him from his goal: that of destruction and death.

Hector wondered whether the hog was experiencing the same acute pain in its throat and lungs as he was from running. It was hardly an equal contest; four legs were surely better than two. His fevered imagination was certain that he could feel the hog's hot breath on the back of his legs. At any moment he expected the beast's bony skull to butt him from behind. He could imagine how it would feel to fall on to the damp, earthy forest floor and to be trampled by the devilish trotters of the enraged monster. Frankly, he was surprised that it hadn't happened already. His cloak, a protection from the weather, was now a hindrance during the pursuit. He tried to hold it tight to himself with one hand as he careened through the trees, but brambles and branches reached out and snagged him as he passed. Beneath his flapping cloak the leather pouch knocked against his knees, first the right and then the left, as he pounded on.

Hector's energy was ebbing but at last he could see his horse up ahead. She was nervous, sensing the danger and seeing her master's panic. He grabbed at the reins and leaped into the saddle. He dug his heels into her black flanks and she reared up as he wheeled her round. '*Tartri flammis!*' he muttered, and he reached overhead and snapped off a branch to defend himself, for the snarling, salivating jaws of the monster were heading straight for them.

Suddenly another figure came crashing out from between the trees, waving his arms and shouting. Hector couldn't see the stranger properly (and this was hardly the time to ask for an introduction) but the hog, confused by the commotion, skidded to a halt, flanks heaving, snout dripping. Its head swung back and forth between them as if trying to decide whom to charge, but then it outwitted them both, Hector and the stranger, by running away altogether in completely the other direction.

Hector looked over at the man who was watching as the hog hurtled away into the forest. Still panting from his exertions, he slipped down from his horse and went towards him. 'Thank you,' he said gratefully. 'You saved me.'

'My pleasure,' said the fellow with a slight bow. 'Sometimes one is fortunate to be in the right place at the right time.'

Hector peered out from under his hood at the stranger. There was something familiar about him. His face was in shadow but Hector thought he was older than him if only by a few years. He was not tall, just a few inches above Hector, and his frame was lean.

'How can I repay you?' asked Hector, hoping to delay him a little longer.

The stranger shook his head and waved. 'Don't trouble yourself unduly. Maybe in the future you will be able to do something for me. But now I must get on. Adieu,' he said, and walked away whistling tunefully.

'At least tell me your name,' Hector called after him, but he had already vanished into the trees.

Chapter Twenty

⌒　⌒

Extract from

A Letter to Polly

Withypitts Hall

Dear Polly,

It is past two in the morning but I haven't been to bed yet. First I have to record the events of this evening, share them with someone before I go mad. I apologize for my penmanship, I who instructed you in writing! But my hand still shakes with shock.

The evening started out as every other and I went to the Incunabulorum before retiring. The Feast is drawing ever closer, and I wanted to make sure my charges were well. I am still having trouble sleeping; my mind is in such a state of apprehension these days. I am anxious about the cocoons, my plan and, of course, Bovrik himself. I haven't seen so much of him lately. Lady Mandible keeps him busy and he is back and forth to the City, sometimes away overnight.

The Incunabulorum is distinctly chilly but I find the temperature sharpens my mind. I am haunted by thoughts of my father. I can hardly believe I am so close to avenging him. I tell myself daily upon waking and retiring that I am doing the right thing, that he could not disapprove now.

It eases my mind to keep busy so I began my nightly routine. The cocoons are kept in large glass tanks raised up on wooden blocks. In the space underneath each tank I have placed shallow oil lamps in preparation for hatching. I went from tank to tank and inspected the contents: dozens of pale brown Papilio ingenspennatus cocoons hanging from the lines of thread strung across the interior of each tank. They are all as long as, though fatter than, my thumb, and the threads bow under their weight. I lingered a little longer at the tank in the dimmest corner of the room. The cocoons within are much darker. If only, I thought, Father was here to see them . . .

I am well acquainted with lavishness, that of Withypitts Hall and Urbs Umida, but when I gaze upon these simple miracles of nature I know I am seeing a different kind of beauty to that of Lady Mandible's glittering jewels or Bovrik's ostentatious garb.

Pah! That man! He deserves everything that is coming to him.

When the clock struck midnight I was glad to be startled out of my dark thoughts. After the final bell I was certain I heard a sound in the corridor. My first thought? Bovrik! Who else would be sneaking around at this hour? I opened the door ever so slightly and peered out. I could see no one, just hear the sound of fading footsteps, but it was definitely him. I could smell his lemon-scented trail.

I took off in pursuit and every so often caught sight of his coat-tails as he went round a corner. I crept along, staying close to the walls, brushing against the hangings and the stuffed animals. As we went on the haunting and discordant strains of Mandible's harpsichord grew louder - he has pledged to play at the Feast but I fear he overreaches himself - until finally we came to Lord Mandible's own rooms. And I watched

Bovrik slip into his bedroom. What was he doing? What riddle was this?

Before I could think any further Bovrik re-emerged into the corridor, his cloak clutched oddly about him, and hurried in the opposite direction. I lost sight of him almost straight away, and, more than a little discomfited, I set off for my own tower.

Yet, Polly, it was not even this bizarre encounter that prompted me to put quill to paper. And I can no longer avoid its telling.

Withypitts Hall is a virtual maze and, it being night and my being so caught up in my thoughts, when I raised my eyes I found myself wandering along corridors I did not recognize, for I had taken a wrong turning. Initially I was unworried but as I walked I began to get the strangest feeling that the walls were actually closing in. Without doubt the ceiling was lower. But I kept going.

This part of the hall was not without Lady Mandible's touch, of course, and all along the walls hung canvases of different sizes. They were paintings, but a far cry from the portraits of Mandible ancestors that gaze down sternly elsewhere in Withypitts. Portraits and landscapes in muted pigments, I thought, but done in such a unique way that it was difficult to make out exactly what was being portrayed. I saw beasts and people and skies and sea, but there were other parts I could not understand. The identity of the artist was not such a puzzle. In the corner of each work was clearly marked the word Lysandra. Somehow it did not surprise me that Lady Mandible would portray the world in this way.

As I went further down the corridor the tone of the paintings changed. In the poor light of my reducing candle they began to take on a life of their own. The swirls of dull colour now appeared to me as monstrosities and demons in a hellish inferno. What sort of mind had dreamed up these images?

I saw a door ahead and, despite my many misgivings, curiosity won out and I placed my hand on the knob and began to turn. My heart beat faster. Now I feared as much that which was behind me as what was ahead. The door opened silently and smoothly. I stepped through and heard it close again with a soft click.

I was standing in a large room. Moonlight shone through the window to my left and a dying fire breathed its last in the fireplace opposite. The room was lavishly furnished, but on account of the light everything seemed

grey. Tentatively I made my way between the dark
silhouettes towards the fireplace. To the left of it
stood a wooden easel draped with a cloth, a canvas
beneath, and beside it a low table with jars and brushes
and a palette almost wholly smeared with thick blobs of
colour. I took a brush and examined it. 'Hog bristle,' I
thought, 'to furnish Lady Mandible's hobby.' For in my mind
there was no doubt that this was her room. I almost
lifted the cover off the canvas but stopped. I had
little desire to look upon it if it was the same as those
I had passed in the corridor.

Then I heard a sigh. I was not alone.

Slowly I turned towards the sound and saw for
the first time, on a low divan under the window, a body.
I watched, frozen to the spot, but it didn't move. I
crept closer, keeping low behind the furniture. I could
see now that it was a man. His head rested on a pillow
and his eyes were closed. He wore no shirt and in the
moonlight his white chest almost glowed.

It was Gerulphus. He appeared to be asleep.
He was breathing deeply, his chest rising and falling
evenly, so I ventured even closer and saw that he
was covered in large, dark marks. They were thick

and raised and, though I could hardly believe it, moving.

Because they were alive.

'Tartri flammis!' I murmured, and fought the urge to retch, for Gerulphus's chest and stomach were covered in black, bloated, blood-sucking leeches!

What strange practice is this? I asked myself, and spun about to leave. But to my utter horror I heard footsteps, a hand on the door and a voice that sent a chill through my heart.

'Gerulphus? Are you there?'

I ran to duck behind a chair, hoping that my thunderous heart would not give me away, and watched Lady Mandible enter.

She was dressed all in black with a long peacock-feather boa draped around her shoulders and hanging down her back. Bell-shaped sleeves covered her hands almost to her fingertips. As she moved I could hear the soft swish of her gown. Her lips looked dark purple in the light. She went straight to Gerulphus and poked him with a beringed digit. The manservant started visibly and opened his eyes.

'Have they finished?'

Gerulphus looked down at his chest and nodded slowly. So Lady Mandible reached out with her long nails to slide them between the leeches and the manservant's chest, detaching the engorged creatures one by one. Her mouth was open in a half-smile as she carried out this grisly task – I am certain that she was enjoying every moment. The leeches (I counted twenty in all) were placed in a large jar on the table beside them. No wonder Gerulphus looked so pale, I thought; he must be almost bloodless.

'Excellent,' Lady Mandible purred. 'Prepare them for me to use the blood tomorrow,' and she left the room with barely a backward glance.

Gerulphus stood up and slowly pulled on his shirt. His wounds were oozing blood and soon the white cloth was red-stained but he seemed to take no notice. To my great relief he too left the room minutes later (at least I didn't have to see what horrors the 'preparation' would entail) and at last I felt secure enough to come out from my hiding place. I went back to the easel and slowly pulled up the cloth. I stared at the half-finished canvas and saw not the horned demons or the one-eyed monsters or the fork-tongued devils, but only the reddish brown with which they were painted. And I wondered for the first time what I was doing here, in a place where the bristles of a brush were dipped in human blood . . .

Chapter Twenty-One

A Tuneful Interlude

Lord Mandible tutted and took Percy from the harpsichord, kissed him on the nose and put him gently on the floor. 'Go find your precious sister; go find Posset,' he crooned. The cat trotted away as Lord Mandible flicked out his coat-tails and carefully placed his ample silk-clad bottom on the ruby-hued leather stool. It was not so easy to sit down, what with his stiff leg and his straining buttons. He blamed Mrs Malherbe's pies. He knew he should refrain, but they were just too delicious.

With some degree of affectation he flexed and cracked his fingers, then began to play the elegant instrument in front of him. It was an Italian harpsichord, made by the renowned Funiculi brothers in Rome, and his father had played it exquisitely right up until the moment of his death – quite literally, the poor man having collapsed and died across the keyboard. It was in memory of his father that Mandible had taken up the instrument, but he lacked his father's talent. He played vigorously but badly (not that his tutor, standing to one side, would ever dare tell him so).

'Your Lordship,' he said at the end of the tune, 'may I commend you on playing every note!' For it was true, Mandible had played every note, just not necessarily in the order or pitch suggested on the sheet. 'It is no longer possible to draw comparisons between your playing and that of my other pupils,' he continued with a set smile. 'You are without doubt in a class of your own.'

This pleased Mandible greatly.

'But, a note of caution, Your Lordship,' warned the tutor. 'I know you wish to play at the Midwinter Feast but I am not sure the untrained ears of your guests are ready for your particular facility.'

As if he hadn't even spoken, Mandible declared, 'The Midwinter Feast will be the perfect opportunity to demonstrate my talent. I have been working on a tune, now all I need are the words. Would you like to hear it?'

The tutor nodded and, resigned to the inevitable, comforted himself with the thought that of all the nights of the year for Mandible to play, the night of the Midwinter Feast was probably the best. If previous years were anything to go by, the revellers would be so drunk so quickly that, to their thickened ears, sweet music could be wrung from a strangled cat.

A knock on the door was followed closely by the entrance of Gerulphus. 'Lady Mandible wishes to see you, Your Lordship,' he hissed.

'Just when I was getting to grips with it too!' muttered Mandible. 'Does she not realize I'm busy?'

'She insists.'

What Lysandra had actually said was, 'If that fool is fiddling upon his harpsichord again, I don't care if you have to crash the lid on his rubber fingers, though it might improve his playing. Tell him to come here.'

Gerulphus had taken advantage of the long journey from his mistress's quarters to the music room to paraphrase the message. Mandible hurried after him, his limping gait causing his trousers to crepitate rhythmically.

Lady Mandible was perfectly happy for her husband to pursue the harpsichord. It kept him busy and out of her hair (a considerable mass these days according to the latest style) as did his hours of fruitless hog hunting in the forest. It was better than the days immediately after his father's death, which he had spent weeping and wailing around the Hall, lamenting the fact that he was not the man his father was and never would be. As far as Lysandra was concerned *she* was the man Mandible should have been and it suited her well.

When Lord Mandible arrived at his wife's rooms Lysandra greeted him and held out her hand for his kiss.

'Ah, my dearest one,' he said, for no other reason than manners, and pressed his lips against her ever-cold alabaster skin. 'Might I say you look particularly beautiful today.'

Lady Mandible acknowledged the compliment with a very slight nod, in part because her trio of coiffure maids were in the middle of trying to arrange her curls in the shape of a naval ship complete with rigging.

'My dear,' she said with only the merest hint of disdain (let it not be said that she was not as well brought up as her husband), 'I wanted to ask you something but I was afraid you had already gone hunting.'

'Why, no,' Lord Mandible laughed – a high-pitched titter such as one would expect from a mouse, if a mouse could laugh – and he sat in a chair that he hadn't noticed before (another of Lysandra's recent purchases). 'I was merely amusing myself on my instrument. Did I tell you that my tutor said I had a gift like no other?'

'I can believe that,' she said evenly. 'Certainly *I* have never heard anything quite like it.'

Mandible looked pleased and crossed and uncrossed his legs twice, causing his silk breeches to crackle alarmingly. 'So, what do you wish to ask?'

'I wish to know if you will be providing a Hairy-Backed Hog for the centrepiece of the Midwinter Feast, or if I must send one of our other huntsmen out . . . as usual. It is, after all, only days away.'

'Do not fear, dearest one,' replied Mandible. 'I will be. I am certain my luck is about to change.'

'You might have more luck with that musket of yours if you aimed it at some of those poachers,' said Lysandra drolly. 'I don't think they can run as fast as a hog.' She threw back her head and laughed mockingly, causing a minor panic among her fretting maids. Going on past performance she was doubtful of her husband's claim, despite his boneheaded perseverance and optimism. But she could never resist an opportunity to remind her husband of his inadequacies.

Lord Mandible hurried from their meeting, the sound of her harsh laughter still ringing in his ears. He'd show her and make his father proud. He was determined to catch a hog. The previous night he had enjoyed a marvellous dream of the Midwinter Feast. He sat at one end of the dining table in the great hall staring straight into the dead eyes of a roasted, glistening Hairy-Backed Hog, and its expression seemed to say, 'You won, Your Lordship. You got me at last.'

The fantasy culminated in a riotous toast and when Mandible awoke his ears were still ringing with the clashing of silver goblets and the cheering of nobles. And dreams can come true with a little forward planning! At the next opportunity he would speak to that butterfly boy, he decided. It was well known around the Hall that he was always available for extra work.

Lady Mandible shooed her maids irritably from her room and went through to her bedchamber. She lay back on her bed and gazed fixedly at the silvery gauze canopy above her, her mouth turned up slightly at the corners, pondering the question of the Baron.

It caused her to sigh deeply.

Without a doubt he was a charming fellow with a ready

wit and handsome face, if a rather angular profile, but could he be trusted? She had decided not. She did not regret engaging him – he had been very useful to her – and his funny eye-tricks and garish outfits amused her, but Bovrik was reaching the end of his useful life. His desire to please, his devotion and sedulous nature could no longer outweigh how intensely aggravating she now found him. Constantly at her side, always agreeing with her and stroking the velvet drapes, or running his hand over the rugs whilst exuding that ghastly lemon smell over everything. She was tired of it. And that look in his one good eye when she refused him something, like a puppy that had been kicked. Ugh! She couldn't bear it. It made him weak. The thought made her shudder. She would never have got to where she was today if she had been so feeble. But even worse – he was stealing from her! Well, did he really think she wouldn't notice? Gerulphus had noted everything he had taken.

Yes, there was no question about it, Bovrik would have to go and he would pay for his treachery. But all in good time and not before the Feast. Nothing was to spoil that. Until then he might still be useful. He was so good at anticipating her . . . tastes. Thinking of the Feast made Lysandra smile. It was her first as mistress of Withypitts,

and she was determined it would be one to remember. She
couldn't deny that Bovrik's suggestion of a re-enactment of
Trimalchio's Feast was a stroke of genius. But the *pièce de
résistance*, the butterflies, was her idea and hers alone. No
one would know what it was until the day!

Absentmindedly she reached out and picked up the
latest edition of the *Diurnal Journal,* which had arrived that
morning. A headline caught her eye: 'Handsome Heir to
Eastern Throne Arrives in Urbs Umida to Much Fanfare'.
How interesting! She really must pop into town again soon
and see what all the fuss was about. Just then, the tinkle of
a bell told her that Gerulphus had arrived in the next room
with her lunch tray.

'Now, there's someone I can truly trust, mostly anyway,'
she said aloud. Yes, mostly, because Lady Mandible judged
everyone as harshly as she judged herself, and she trusted
herself least of all.

Chapter Twenty-Two

An Interesting Request

It was early evening and Hector sat in his tower room, busy with his pestle and mortar. It was only a matter of days since he had followed the Baron and endured the incident with the leeches but, although he hadn't forgotten it (or the dreadful journey back to his room), he was not going to allow it to deter him from his true purpose. He owed it to his father.

With the Feast imminent there was an atmosphere of great excitement and anticipation in every room and corridor, which only heightened Hector's own apprehension.

A large moth flapped at his windowpane. Hector looked out at it, into the darkness, and was surprised to see a flickering light high up in the building opposite.

'It must be in the other tower,' he thought, 'but that's empty.'

'Master Hector?'

The voice came from directly outside the room but Hector knew immediately who it was. There was only one person in Withypitts Hall who could climb the stone staircase up to his room without making a sound: the inscrutable Gerulphus.

'Come in,' he called, and the next minute the skeletal manservant appeared around the door. The candlelight seemed to exaggerate the shadows under his eyes and his hollow cheeks. If Hector hadn't known him, he might have thought him a ghoul.

'Lady Mandible wishes to see you.' Gerulphus looked towards the mortar. 'Something for the butterflies?'

'Er . . . yes,' said Hector, and he covered it with a cloth.

'Does it stain? I see you are wearing gloves.'

'It does,' said Hector, and he pulled off the gloves, leaving them inside out. He tied his cuffs, which he had loosened earlier, and ran his fingers through his hair to flatten it before leaving the room and locking the door.

Gerulphus led the way briskly. When they crossed the

entrance hall the manservant, as usual, made hardly a sound. But Hector was acutely aware of the tap-tap of his own leather-heeled boots on the black and white marbled floor. Finally, Gerulphus drew up at Lady Mandible's suite, before a huge set of ebony double doors, and indicated to Hector that he should wait outside. As soon as the door shut fully Hector put his ear against the glossy wood, but he could not hear a thing and was caught off guard when Gerulphus suddenly opened the door again and ushered him in.

Hector found himself standing in semi-darkness in a large, high-ceilinged room. He waited for his eyes to adjust to the gloom. Around the room the walls were covered in bookshelves, and between them, in arched alcoves, stood black marble statues of everything from classical busts to fat, cross-legged imps. The only light came from a couple of polished girandoles on the far side of the room.

'Hector?'

Lady Mandible was standing at the fireplace. This evening she was dressed from head to toe in purple velvet and her black hair gleamed. Large jewels at her throat and wrists and rings on her fingers coruscated in the firelight. She beckoned to him with a painted talon.

With each step Hector's foot sank into the deep pile of

the rug. He was near enough to feel the heat of the fire when he saw something that stopped him dead.

'Oh!' he breathed, the wind knocked out of him. For there on the wall above the mantelpiece was the entire collection of his father's mounted butterflies.

'How on earth . . . ?' he whispered, and involuntarily his hand reached up to the cocoon he wore around his neck.

'Magnificent, aren't they?' said Lady Mandible, her voice smooth as silk and twice as slippery. Hector felt her hand on his shoulder and fancied he could feel its chill even through his waistcoat and shirt.

'I believe they belonged to a gentleman who had fallen on hard times,' she went on. 'Bovrik found them for me in the City. And as soon as he told me of them I had an idea of what I would do to make the Midwinter Feast special this year.'

Hector remembered the crate Bovrik had taken from Badlesmire and Leavelund. What a twist of fate, he thought. He could hardly believe that it was not simply butterflies, his father's beloved hobby, that had brought him here and enabled his chance at revenge, but his father's very own butterfly collection itself. Surely it was meant to be.

'Collecting like this, it is called lepidoptery,' said Hector quietly. 'From the Greek word *lepidos*, meaning fish scale, on account of the scales on butterfly wings. They reflect light to give them their colour.'

Lady Mandible regarded him closely. 'Once again you surprise me with your learning, young Hector.' By means of a sharp fingernail in the small of his back, she guided him firmly to a chair and sat herself opposite. 'And what of my butterflies? You know I am relying on you to make the Feast an evening to remember.'

'They will be ready.' Hector shuddered at the intensity of her mesmerizing gaze. He couldn't shake the feeling that she knew far more about him than he had ever told. But that was silly . . .

'None of this is why I called you to me, however. I have heard via the servants that you are quite a riddler.' She smiled graciously. 'Well, I need you to write a riddle for me. It must be very clever, but that is no problem for you.'

Despite himself, Hector felt momentarily flattered.

'That's easy, My Lady.' He thought for a moment, then took the quill and thick cream-coloured paper she pushed across the small table between them. Quickly, he wrote one of his favourite riddles down, taking extra care with his letters. It could not fail to impress her, he was sure. He folded the paper and passed it back.

Lysandra rose, an indication that it was time for Hector to go. As she turned from him she unfolded the piece of paper and began to read.

As Hector went on his way he thought he heard a voice calling from outside. He went to the nearest window and looked out to see a figure in the dark and snowy courtyard below. Lord Mandible! It had to be. The way he dragged his bad leg was unmistakable. Hector strained to hear what he was saying and finally made out a forlorn word, being called over and over.

'Posset! Posset!'

He shook his head in disbelief for the hundredth time since his arrival. What a strange place this Hall was.

Chapter Twenty-Three

Betrayal

Hector climbed the winding stone stairs that led to the top of one of the six towers that formed each corner of the hexagonal Withypitts Hall walls, more specifically the tower where he had seen the flickering light earlier that evening, a light he was determined to investigate. As he climbed he tried to put his strange meeting with the fascinating Lady Mandible from his mind.

The stairs wound around the inside of the tower, leaving a huge darkened chasm in the middle. About halfway up, a three-tiered candelabrum was suspended on a long thick chain, exactly the same as in his own tower and in the more luxurious, less filthy turret that the fiendish Baron inhabited.

The daily job of lighting the thick candles and lanterns about the Hall was supposed to be done by the small kitchen boy. It was a job he undertook with great reluctance because it involved leaning out over railings and banisters with a hooked stick and pulling the light fitting towards him with one hand while using the other to light the wicks. And as with most things in Withypitts, Lady Mandible had ordered the most expensive and elaborate light fixtures available. The complicated design of her chandeliers and candelabra only added to their weight as well as beauty. By the time he finished the boy's arms would be shaking from the effort, and having no head for heights many a near fall had left him in a cold sweat, particularly in the weeks leading up to the Feast.

What the boy couldn't know was that almost since his arrival at the Hall Hector had been shortening the hooked stick, thus causing him to lean out further and further each time. And a few days previously, Hector had judged the time right and approached the boy to offer to do this job for him, in return for a small part of his wage. He agreed readily. Hector had felt bad about this deceit, but he told himself he had no choice – a greater cause was at stake. Being the lamplighter enabled him to walk all the corridors and towers of Withypitts without arousing suspicion. In this way he could keep an eye on things, in particular the Baron's quarters. And the extra money was not to be sneezed at as the Feast and his departure immediately after approached.

So now Hector climbed the empty tower, stick and taper in hand as a ready excuse if anyone should find him there. At the top of the steps was a stout door with a sliding panel, in it and a huge padlock hanging from the handle. Cautiously, he put his ear to the door but there wasn't a sound within. Light came from the gaps around the panel, however, so Hector took a deep breath, slid it across carefully and peered in.

A hatted figure lay on a small bed on the far side of the room which was otherwise almost bare. The fellow looked remarkably at ease under the circumstances, with his hands behind his head, and as Hector watched he began to whistle softly, a tune that Hector recognized, and tipped his hat backwards.

Hector gave a gasp. He knew who this whistling youth was; he was the young man who had saved his life in the forest, the very same chap who, for some reason, was so familiar to him.

'Ho there!' the youth called out, sitting up as Hector's

gasp alerted him to his presence. 'Welcome to my chamber.'

'What are you doing here?' Hector asked. 'Why are you locked in?'

'My own fault,' the cheery fellow responded. He rose from the bed and came over to the door, his green eyes peering at Hector through the hole. 'I should have known better than to loiter in the forest. Lord Mandible came upon me when he was hunting and was convinced I was poaching his hogs.'

Hector found himself wanting to apologize. For some reason he felt responsible for the stranger's misfortune, though he wasn't sure why. 'I don't understand why you're so cheerful,' he said eventually instead. 'Aren't you at least scared or angry? Don't you want to get out of here?'

'I'm sure things will work themselves out for the best.' The young man smiled enigmatically then gave Hector a significant look. 'I find it is healthier to forgive and forget than to harbour darker thoughts. The sweetness of revenge soon turns sour, I have learned, and its aftertaste may never leave you.' He paused. 'By the look on your face, I would hazard a guess you have a secret of your own to share, and I have plenty of time to listen . . . '

Hector felt his jaw drop. What could this strange young

man know about him or his past to make such insightful remarks? But before he could say another word the stranger continued. His tone was mournful, but there was a twinkle in his eye. 'Who knows how long I shall be held up here? There's no way out except by the padlocked door through which I came.'

Hector chewed thoughtfully on his lip, mindful of the debt of life he owed this blithe prisoner. If there was only a way to liberate him from this dreadful prison, his debt would be repaid. He glanced down at the unyielding padlock. Even if he could open it, it would be such a risk. He could jeopardize his chance of revenge against Bovrik and he couldn't let that happen. 'Well, there's not much I can do about that,' he forced himself to say evenly.

The young man grinned, seemingly unperturbed. 'As I have said before, there is a time for everything and now is not the time.'

But before Hector could ask what he meant by that the stranger put a finger to his lips. 'Shh!' he hissed. 'Someone's coming.'

Sure enough there was the sound of voices from further down the tower stairs. Then Lady Mandible and Bovrik appeared around the turn, with a guardsman beside them.

Hector forced himself to stand calmly by the door as the duo approached. Besides, it was not possible to descend the stairs with them before him. Today the Baron wore scarlet and yellow, with silver-buckled shoes. He preened his waxed moustache eagerly. His obvious, excessive attempts to ensure his appearance reinforced his faked titled identity greatly amused Hector. Does he really think a true baron would draw attention to himself in such a way? thought Hector. It was laughable.

'Hector!' Lady Mandible declared with apparent delight when she saw him, while the Baron frowned. 'What do you here?'

Hector held up his taper in answer.

'Well, it is fortuitous indeed. Would you not like to see what use I have for the information you so kindly provided me with earlier this evening?'

'Er . . .' Hector was baffled.

'I wonder what you are up to, My Lady. I wonder too that you should infolf this . . . this serfant boy before me.' Bovrik smiled as if in jest, but the smile was not broad enough to cause his yellow eyepatch to move. Nonetheless he reached into his pocket, took out a large key and unlocked the padlocked door. Lady Mandible, her eyes sparkling in seeming anticipation, entered the cell with him and Hector slipped in behind them. The guard positioned himself by the open door.

The young prisoner was sitting silently on his bed. Hector admired his cool demeanour but he had a bad feeling about all this.

'So this is the odious poacher your husband discofered,' Bovrik stated in his heavy accent. 'Shall I arrange for him to be transported to Urbs Umida and thrown in Irongate prison to rot?'

'I am not a poacher,' said the young man. 'I was merely passing through.'

Lady Mandible ignored them both.

'Young fellow,' she said instead, 'I have a proposition for you. I would not wish it said that I do not give a man a fair chance so I have decided that if you can answer this riddle, you may go free. If you cannot . . . the punishment for your crimes will be dire.'

Bovrik raised his eyebrows while Hector took a sharp intake of breath. Had he heard her right? Did she say riddle? Surely not *his* riddle! He watched in disbelief as she handed Bovrik a piece of paper, the very same paper Hector had given Her Ladyship not an hour since.

'Baron, read it out for us to hear,' she commanded.

Bovrik sneered at the prisoner. 'It is My Lady's wish that you answer this riddle to ensure your freedom.'

'Very well,' he replied steadily, getting to his feet. 'I enjoy a challenge.'

Hector covered his face with his hands.

'Consider this,' began Bovrik. 'A man is trafelling in a land where the people are either liars or truth-tellers. He comes to a fork in the road. He knows that one road leads to poisonous marshes where he will suffer a painful and prolonged death if he breathes in the marsh gases; the other leads to his destination, a beautiful city. There is no sign and he doesn't know which way to go. He sits at the crossroads and efentually two men come down the road to meet him. One of them is a truth-teller, and one of them is a liar but the trafeller does not know which is which. He is allowed to ask only one question to find the way to go. The trafeller thinks for a moment and then he asks a simple question and soon afterwards he is on his way to the city.

'The riddle is this,' said Bovrik with a quick look at Lady Mandible who was listening eagerly, her hands clasping and unclasping, her rings flashing. 'What was the question and whom did he ask?'

Hector's heart was in his mouth. If only he had known what Lady Mandible was planning! But flattered by her attention, drawn in by her cold beauty, he had not even asked the riddle's purpose. Instead, he had taken great pride in making it as complicated as he could. He had been used. And now this innocent man was to suffer. 'When you run with wolves, you become a wolf,' he muttered to himself, remembering again his father's last words. And he felt for the first time a proper twinge of doubt. These thoughts, along with the smug look on Lady Mandible's face as she enjoyed the power she held in her hands at this moment with her tasteless game, made bile rise in Hector's throat.

But then the prisoner spoke. 'The answer is simple, kind sir,' he said with a small bow laced with a generous amount of sarcasm. He then calmly proceeded to give the correct response.

As he did so, Hector finally realized what was so familiar about this young man: *his voice*. He was the rhyming riddler from the square in Urbs Umida. Hector was aghast. Could he have been following him this whole time, he wondered, as he remembered too the shadowy figure in Pagus Parvus who had seemed to be watching him? Surely he wasn't that keen for his answer to 'The Landlord's Pickle'? What was this fellow up to?

Bovrik reddened in anger as he read the same answer on the paper before him. Hector could barely conceal his relief, despite his wonder at the strange coincidence of his repeated encounters with this riddler. Then he saw Lady Mandible's face, an impassive mask. Would he be in trouble now?

But when she caught his eye she merely shrugged and said, 'Interesting. He's cleverer than I first thought.' Turning away again she added, 'Leave the poacher here anyway.'

Hector swallowed a protest. The prisoner obviously did not know so well.

'But Your Ladyship,' he said quietly, 'I answered correctly. You said I should then be allowed to go free.'

'I've changed my mind,' said Lysandra flippantly as she swept from the room, 'just because I can.'

Bovrik followed, shooting Hector another dirty look as he passed. Hector glanced desperately at the accused and watched helplessly as, once they had all exited the cell, Bovrik locked the door with obvious delight and stationed the guard there. Would Hector ever be able to uncover the mystery behind this unflappable stranger?

At the bottom of the tower stairs, as Lady Mandible and the Baron walked away from him, a hand grabbed Hector by the shoulder and spun him around. He found himself staring straight into the eyes of Lord Mandible.

'Hector?' he said.

'Yes.'

'I have a job for you.'

Chapter Twenty-Four

Musings

Baron Bovrik de Vandolin, still chewing on his breakfast, took out his box of eyeballs and set it down on his desk. He opened the lid and his smile widened when he saw what lay within: six staring eyeballs arranged in order of acquisition. The second from last, inset with an emerald, had been purchased using the proceeds of the sale of a small silver plate he had found in a dark corner of a far corridor and the last, jade, by means of a medieval toasting goblet.

'Only one more,' thought Bovrik, 'and the set will be complete.'

He took them out one by one and polished them with a soft cloth before replacing them so they all stared in the same direction. It was a daily ritual. Only then would he decide which to wear. Today he chose the third across. Its pearly pupil would go nicely with his waistcoat. With a swift and practised movement, a duck and a shake of the head, the chosen eyeball was in. He hoped it would please Lady Mandible and now that was more important than ever.

Bovrik sighed deeply when he thought of her and sat heavily in his chair. He clutched the velvet cushion to himself and frowned. He couldn't deny it any longer: Lady Mandible had changed towards him. He had not failed to notice lately how many messages were relayed to him via that dratted Gerulphus rather than personally. And had she not made her plans for that poacher without involving him at all until the last moment? But what had changed? Surely she could not have found out about his true identity? No, that was impossible. It had to be something else. He had grown used to this life of abundance. Sometimes he actually shivered as he walked Withypitts' corridors, such was the wondrous effect on him of their luxury. To Bovrik, living at Withypitts Hall was the closest thing to heaven he thought a person could experience on earth. And it was certainly as close to heaven as he would ever get, being bound for hell at the earliest opportunity.

Increasingly, he found himself choosing to ignore his old maxim 'A good swindler knows when to go'. And now, instead of taking Lady Mandible's change towards him as proof of his very own saying, he chose instead to seek ways to make himself indispensible and secure his future at the Hall. He went to his desk and withdrew a leaflet from the drawer. He read it through again and laughed. It was something he had come across during a recent foray in the City. To be honest it had repelled him slightly, but now it occurred to him it might be something she would appreciate. The time had come to make use of it. It could only raise him in her estimation. And he had his own plans for the Feast too . . . The truth of it, he had to admit, was there was only one way he could stay forever. If he could just get rid of Lord Mandible, perhaps eventually *he*, Baron Bovrik de Vandolin, could step into his shoes . . .

Excitedly Bovrik snatched up his Jocastar cloak and buried his face in it. Reassured once more as to his baron-like appearance, suddenly everything seemed possible – even the highly improbable!

Chapter Twenty-Five

A Premature Arrival

A very slight noise, a noise he wasn't supposed to hear, caused Hector to stop what he was doing and to listen. Could he be imagining it? No, there it was again. A fluttering sound. No doubt about it. He could feel his palms moistening. There shouldn't be any fluttering. It was too early. The Feast wasn't until tomorrow evening. He put down the mortar and turned around. He walked slowly up and down the trestles, looking for the source of the sound. A movement on the floor of the tank beside him caused him to exclaim loudly, '*Tartri flammis!*'

His hands flew up to his mouth as he watched in horror the large butterfly that was flapping around there, disturbing the layers of damp bark and dark earth. He hadn't noticed it at rest earlier, because its vibrant colours were smeared and acted as camouflage, hiding it in the debris. Its body was large but its wings were horribly malformed, one quite literally torn to shreds, the other a crumpled mess. With fast-beating heart Hector opened the door and reached in to retrieve the struggling creature. It hauled itself painfully on to his palm and sat quietly resting as he withdrew it.

Hector felt both pity and revulsion at the same time. Anxiously he examined the interior of the tank again. This butterfly seemed to be the only one that had hatched out. Perhaps it wasn't as bad as he had at first thought. This one couldn't survive though. But even in its agony, it seemed a terrible thing to do to kill it. So Hector hesitated and did not see until too late the shadow that was cast over him like an engulfing monster.

'What haf you got there?'

Bovrik's voice caused Hector to half leap out of his skin. He turned quickly and found himself staring directly into the glinting pupil of the fake Baron's false eye.

Bovrik was mildly surprised at Hector's reaction. It was rare he saw the boy discomposed in this way. In fact, Hector displayed little emotion around him. He moved closer, a smile of curiosity playing around his mouth. The ends of his moustache twitched.

'What is it?'

'It's . . . it's a butterfly,' stammered Hector. Immediately Bovrik's face darkened and his eyebrows knitted together.

'A butterfly? Already?'

'I know,' said Hector, looking down at the quivering creature. 'It has come out early.'

'That much is apparent,' said Bovrik coldly.

'It's injured; it cannot survive.'

'Are there any others?'

'No.'

'Hmm,' murmured Bovrik, and he walked slowly around the room examining the cocoons. 'These are different.' He was standing by the tank in the corner. The cocoons within were smaller and much darker.

'Just another species,' said Hector. 'To add some variation.'

Bovrik remained silent.

'I can bring the rest out when they are needed,' said Hector evenly, always surprised at how easily he disguised his utter contempt for the man.

'Let's hope so. And what of this?' Now Bovrik was holding up the mortar.

Hector darted over to him and took it back. 'It's for the butterflies. You mustn't touch it.'

Bovrik looked at him sharply. 'You know what you are doing, I suppose,' he said finally. 'Far be it from me to interfere.' He completed his circuit and came to stand in front of Hector again. 'But nothing more can be allowed to go wrong. Things must be perfect for Her Ladyship.' Then, almost under his breath Hector thought he heard him add, 'Especially now.' The Baron pointed at him. 'Show it to me,' he demanded.

Hector held out his hand and Bovrik took another look at the struggling butterfly.

'I suppose one is not such a tragedy,' he said, and then without warning he snatched it up and squeezed it within his closed fist until its innards oozed out from between his fingers. Hector stifled a gasp, taken aback by the savagery of his action. Bovrik opened his hand and held it out to Hector.

'Get rid of it,' he said.

Hector swallowed hard. Slowly he pulled the dead insect off by a wing and placed it on the table.

You monster! he thought with a ferocity he hadn't known was in him. His heart felt squeezed dry, but he did not allow his expression to betray him.

'I don't have time for any more mistakes, boy. I have far more important things to attend to. Remember, I found you on the streets of Urbs Umida. I can put you back there.'

'And I, you,' Hector whispered to himself as he watched Bovrik turn on his heel and hurry out. 'Or worse.'

Chapter Twenty-Six

A Letter to Polly

Dear Polly,

I hardly know where to start. I am filled with disguist at how I allowed myself to be used to punish the prisoner, to nearly bring about his death. That is Lady Mandible's strength. In her presence men become weak, and I am not even a man. And I am still sickened at the thought of the crushed butterfly in Bovrik's palm.

However, I must warn you now, if you thought Gerulphus and his leeches were sufficiently repulsive, or that Lady Mandible's paintings in blood were no less

than an abomination, then cover your eyes and read no
further.

Only horror lies ahead. I have just witnessed a
most disturbing theatre.

After Bovrik left the Hatchery in such a rush, I
followed him. I could not help thinking that a man in such
a hurry was worth keeping an eye on.

This time I was determined not to lose him.
The hour was already late and not many servants still
frequented the halls, so I was able to follow without
detection. Eventually, after many twists and turns, we
came to a small, narrow corridor. I thought it was a dead
end. A tapestry hung on the far wall, but Bovrik drew it
aside to reveal a door, through which he passed quickly.
I ran lightly to the door and knelt at the keyhole to
see within.

Polly, how I wish now that I had not, for some
memories may never be erased!

Lady Mandible sat in a dark chair and Bovrik stood
to her side. A third person, a man, stood before them.
Together the loathsome pair watched, as did I from
my secret place, in speechless, fascinated revulsion.
The whole episode took perhaps twenty minutes, maybe

a little more, and it was done. And well done, if such a thing is possible. The man, a Frenchman I think, stood in the centre of the room as if on a stage and held the animal delicately by its rear legs in his long thin fingers, in the same way one would hold a chicken drumstick. He bit at it, and not at all tentatively as one might expect. He looked as if he might actually enjoy the taste. As he chewed, the tufts of fur caught at the corner of his mouth trembled until the tip of his tongue darted out and pulled them in. The smaller bones crunched between his teeth, the larger ones he sucked clean and then discarded. All the time his expression was one of intense concentration. There was no blood. The creature was obviously already dead. For myself, I suspect that it had been cooked to make it more palatable. Boiled rather than roasted, I found myself thinking in a strangely distanced fashion, for surely if the latter then the fur would have been scorched off, in the same way that the wiry hair of the Hairy-Backed Forest Hog is scorched off before the animal is placed on the spit.

He did not eat the head and I was glad, for there was something about the idea of seeing those velvet triangular white-tipped ears going into the man's mouth that I thought I should not be able to stand. Finally, having reached the end of this grisly meal, he produced from his pocket a large linen napkin with creases as sharp as one of Mrs Malherbe's kitchen knives, and dabbed at his mouth and cleaned his fingers.

Lady Mandible was immediately on her feet and applauding with unfettered enthusiasm. She even clasped Bovrik's hand, if momentarily, and thanked him breathlessly. It was the most emotional I had ever seen her. Bovrik too seemed impressed, though a little paler. Are they so indulged that only such extreme depravities can reach or stir them?

They came towards the door. Quickly I hid in the folds of the tapestry and they passed by me, only inches away. Lady Mandible came first with her bright eyes and those scarlet lips stretched across her pearly teeth. She was laughing. Bovrik was at her side, showing off his latest eyeball. I believe he must have arranged the event for her amusement. The Frenchman followed them both, preening in Lady Mandible's continued praise.

Presumably the bizarre performer was paid a great

deal. I imagine that would be the first requirement if one was expected to . . . to eat a cat as entertainment. For that is what he had just done, Polly. I am sickened and ashamed that I stayed to watch. Surely I was not like this before this twisted place! Surely the Hector of old would have long turned away, just as he would not leave an innocent man to fester in a tower, however difficult it might be to reach him.

But, Polly, the worst of it was, the cat was Posset!

And there is yet more to come. Still in a daze I entered the vacant room. In the dim light I made my way to Lady Mandible's chair; it was warm to the touch, and I lowered myself into it. I sat back and waited for my nerves to settle. Hardly aware I was doing so, I began to stroke the velvety armrests. It was not smooth leather I felt beneath my fingers but some sort of fur, incredibly soft fur. With growing unease I ran my hand to the end of the armrest. The texture suddenly changed. Now it was hard and unyielding. I could feel knuckles and joints and fingers. For a brief moment I was paralysed with horror. Then I leaped up from my seat with a stifled scream.

The Eyeball Collector

I had been sitting in the grotesque beast chair of which Oscar Carpue had spoken in Pagus Parvus. I stumbled towards the fireplace, my heart thudding, only to be confronted with another appalling manifestation. Over the mantel, where I should have expected a looking glass, I saw instead a hunting trophy. But it was not a stag or a hog, it was the beast's head. His cold, soulless eyes stared down at me and I felt an indescribable sadness.

Every time I think I have seen the worst this abominable place has to offer, I am proved wrong. As for the despicable man who plays at baron, I can hardly wait until the Feast is over and my task is completed. Then I shall be gone from here, for I swear, if I have to stay a moment longer, I fear for my sanity and my character.

At last it is time to bestir the butterflies and begin my plan in earnest.

Salve,

Your friend,

Hector

Part the Third

The Midwinter Feast

Extract from the Menu at
Trimalchio's Feast (c. AD 65)

Gustatio accompanied by **honeyed wine**
Sweet dormice sprinkled with honey and poppy seeds
Plums and pomegranate seeds
Small birds, 'Beccaficos', in spiced egg yolk

Fercula accompanied by **Felarian wine**
Foods of the Zodiac
Aries - chick peas, **Taurus** - beef, **Gemini** - kidneys,
Cancer - crown of myrtle, **Leo** - African figs,
Virgo - sterile sow's womb, **Libra** - scales of tarts and honey cakes,
Scorpio - scorpion fish, **Sagittarius** - eyefish, **Capricorn** - lobster,
Aquarius - goose, **Pisces** - two red mullets
Roasted wild boar with dates suckled by cake
Piglets stuffed with live thrushes
Boiled whole pig stuffed with sausages and black pudding

Mensa Secunda
Pastry thrushes stuffed with raisins and nuts
Quince apples and pork disguised as fowl and fish
Oysters and scallops
Snails

Chapter Twenty-Seven

We're All Going on a Boar Hunt

Down into the kitchens, into the sweat and steam, the hissing and crackling, the spitting and cursing and shouting, the fetching and carrying, the scraping and peeling and chopping and washing and salting and pounding, the squealing and chirping, a young lad came running on the morning of the Midwinter Feast.

'I have news!' he shouted over the din. 'I have news!'

Mrs Malherbe, her face red and shining with perspiration, stopped her stirring. Something in the boy's tone told her that this was news of great import.

'Lord Mandible,' he said, catching his breath.

'What of him?'

'He is back. Look out of the window.'

There was an urgency to the statement that made everyone lay down their knives, spoons and cleavers and rush en masse to the window. They were below ground so their view of the outside world was restricted to a narrow sliver above their heads, but they could see enough. And what they saw made them exclaim.

'Lord above!'

'Mercy!'

'Tickle me with a thorn bush!'

'I don't believe my eyes,' said Mrs Malherbe. Then she turned around to her motley crew. 'Get to it, lads,' she said. 'There's work to be done!'

Few who have been close enough to witness the evil expression of an oncoming Hairy-Back have lived to tell the tale. Its size, its viciousness, its enormous tusks! And with a skull that is two inches thick and cushioned with a thick layer of shock-absorbent cartilage, it is able to run head-on into tree trunks and rocks without injury. No other forest animal could withstand such an impact. This porcine monster is well adapted to its forest home.

It was exactly this sort of beast that Lord Mandible had envisaged on the dining table of his dream. So when the day of the Feast finally dawned he had joined his hunting party at sunrise and gone to the oak forest determined – and oddly confident – that today would be the day.

By the time the group reached the edge of the forest Mandible had managed to settle into his usual uneasy and awkward rhythm on his horse. It was a comical sight and his band of fellow huntsmen amused themselves by taking wagers as to how long he would manage to stay in the saddle and, specifically, which side he would fall from, because they were certain from previous experience that he would be unhorsed eventually.

Mandible was blissfully unaware of the amusement he caused his companions as he rallied them all with great enthusiasm.

'Today is the day, my friends,' he cried. 'On this the occasion of the Midwinter Feast it is imperative that I put a Hairy-Backed Hog on the table. We shall not return until our goal has been achieved.'

Inwardly the huntsmen groaned. They knew how desperately Mandible wanted to catch a hog. They also knew how unlikely it was and could see a long day of fruitless hunting before them.

But if Mandible displayed more confidence than usual it soon seemed he had good reason. The hunting party had just arrived in the forest when they heard rustling and snorting sounds from the undergrowth only feet away from their leader. The huntsmen warned him to be patient (they had seen his hasty technique before), but to no avail.

Mandible levelled his musket in the general direction of the sounds and without warning shot a blast of lead down the barrel into the bushes. It seemed to echo in the forest, as if two shots had been fired, but the hunters hardly had time to consider that, as with an almost human squeal and a roar a bloodied and enraged hog burst out of the bushes and came careering towards Mandible. His horse, having more sense than the rider, turned tail and began to gallop as fast as it could in the opposite direction. Mandible fell off backwards (so no bets were won) and landed flat out on the forest floor. The hog bore down on him at a tremendous speed and in a panic he brandished his musket wildly and fired again. There was a strangely loud bang and to everyone's surprise, Mandible's in particular, the hog stopped in mid-charge, went rigid and keeled over.

All was silent.

'Well done, Your Lordship!' congratulated his chief

huntsman finally, wide-eyed with disbelief. The rest of the group let out a genuine cheer. Mandible himself was still in a state of speechless shock. He scrambled to his feet, aided by a couple of the men, and stood in amazement by the side of the hog.

'I did it!' he breathed. 'I finally did it!'

Genuinely moved, he knelt by the fallen hog. He reached out cautiously to feel its still warm body and a tear or two coursed down his face.

'It's a miracle,' he said softly. 'A miracle. I have bagged the biggest boar in the province! I am a hunter extraordinaire.'

For a moment, he could almost forget his extreme distress about his missing beloved cat. And the entire group of men, some wishing that they too could bag the biggest bore in the province, clapped and cheered in anticipation of an early return to the Hall.

And that is exactly what Mrs Malherbe and her kitchen staff saw when they looked out of the kitchen window: the return of Mandible and his prize. Mandible rode at the head of the procession – for procession it was – with his horse slowed to a trot. At this pace he was able to grip its sides with his knees, hold the reins in one hand and raise the other in triumph. Behind him came the boar, tied by its trotters to a thick branch and carried by four men, two at the front and two at the rear. It was still dripping sticky spit and bodily fluids and blood, leaving a shining wet trail across the courtyard. Bringing up the rear came the remainder of the hunting party, laughing and joking.

'Well, well!' murmured Mrs Malherbe. 'As I live and breathe I never thought to see the day that fellow caught a Hairy-Back.' And Mandible immediately went up in her estimation a little further.

Someone else observed Mandible's triumphant return too. From his Brummagem tower Bovrik watched the procession with a keen eye. So, he has caught a hog at last, he thought. It was a long time since he had seen a whole Hairy-Back that close up . . .

Bovrik raised himself from the chair by his window. At the mirror he examined his shoes and posed with one foot in front of the other, showing off his shapely silk-stockinged calves to their best advantage. He smoothed down his cream velvet knee-length breeches and pulled on his loose-fitting magenta coat. Perfect – he truly looked the part. He finished off with a splash of his lemon perfume.

Finally, Bovrik smiled and opened up his box of eyeballs.

He picked out one between his finger and thumb and held it up to the light.

The seventh eyeball.

Fashioned from white opaque glass, hollow in the middle to lessen its weight, slightly flattened at the top and bottom to ensure a good fit, it might have been similar to those he already had but in fact it was overtly superior. The iris was a band of gold ringed with deep blue sapphires, and the pupil was studded with tiny diamonds that glittered in the light. It was utterly, utterly enchanting and his most expensive to complete the collection. He had an eyeball now for every day of the week and need never make do with an eyepatch again! Surely Lady Mandible would be impressed. And added to the success of that cat-eater it boded well for the future. Roll on the Feast! Then, reassured as to his appearance, he adjusted his frilly cravat, shook out his lacy cuffs, collected his cloak and went back to the narrow window of his tower. But his joy was rudely interrupted. From somewhere in the building came the cacophonous sound of the harpsichord. 'Doesn't that fool have anything better to do?' he muttered. Lord, wouldn't he be glad never to have to suffer that racket again!

Chapter Twenty-Eight

Extract from

A Letter to Polly

Withypitts Hall

Dear Polly,

. . . Oh, Polly, how I wish you could see my butterflies! They are so beautiful, so delicate.

When I last wrote I told you the time had come, then I went to the Incunabulorum and sealed the windows and door. I lit the lamps beneath the tanks and stoked up the fire. And I waited. As the temperature rose I went from tank to tank, looking for signs of life - a tiny movement, a split in a cocoon. But there was nothing. The night wore on. I put more logs on the fire and watched the balls in the thermoscope begin to rise.

And then it happened. In the darkest hour before dawn one of the cocoons began to move. Only slightly at first - I thought I had imagined it - but as the minutes passed it was undeniable. Gradually, one after the other, a split appeared at the head and the butterflies began to emerge.

Polly, they are everything I hoped for and more. Huge, majestic almost, rainbow-coloured, astonishing to behold . . . and then there are my own special ones too . . .

Hector put down his quill and yawned widely. A globule of ink dripped on to his desk and the grey cuff of his shirt soaked it up as if it was thirsty. It was difficult to concentrate when he had been up so many hours on the trot, with so much to do. Outside the daylight was fading fast – another day gone and the Feast about to begin. His bag sat on the bed and beside it a leather purse heavy with coins. Lord Mandible might be strange in many ways but at least he had proved to be grateful and generous. When he had come up to Hector after the episode in the tower, and asked him to aid in the capture of a Hairy-Back, Hector had quickly agreed – the money was too good to refuse. And a splendid job he had done too! By the time Hector had reached the forest early this very morning, as instructed, an extremely large and incredibly dozy Hairy-Back (perhaps the very one he had had the pleasure of meeting before) had already been captured, thanks to some cleverly baited acorns and mushrooms, and penned in the bushes. Hector had released the creature just as the hunting party rode in. Then he had managed, as planned, to shoot the creature at almost exactly the same moment as Mandible's own musket had discharged. When the hog unexpectedly kept going he had even shot it again. Both times the huntsmen thought it was Mandible's own weapon that had brought the animal down. It couldn't have worked out better.

Hector had not bargained, however, on sustaining a wound himself. The first squeal the hunting party heard hadn't been the hog's, it had been his. But he was lucky. It was only a graze to the side of his face, caused by Mandible's musket ball as it flew past him. He still felt a little dizzy though, and now he put his hand to the wound on his forehead. He winced, but weighed again the purse in his hand. It was worth it. This money, along with the mysterious ring he had found in the forest (he could feel it in his waistcoat pocket at this very moment), would certainly help him on his way. For once he left the Hall what would he have other than the satisfaction that came with the ultimate revenge? Only the contents of his bag: a couple of books, some clothes and his unsent letters. He planned first to go to Urbs Umida and pay to have his father buried in a better grave. Then he would visit Polly, but after that his future was in the hands of fate.

He pulled on a pair of gloves. On the floor in the corner of the room sat the single glass case wherein quietly rested twenty newly hatched specimens of *Pulvis funestus*, each black as night and sipping daintily from dishes of syrup. He reached for the mortar beside the tank and pulled off the cover.

'Now,' he whispered, 'hold still.'

Not long after, Hector set to work rapidly boxing Lady Mandible's huge and colourful butterflies in time for her to see them before the Feast. He was soon sweating profusely from the effort of his exertions in the steamy Incunabulorum, but more from fear. The moment of truth was drawing ever closer.

The insects were sluggish, having drunk their fill of syrup, and easily caught. Before long Hector was loading the boxes one by one on to a low wheeled trolley. He was just lifting the last one on when there was a knock on his door. He opened it to find Gerulphus waiting to take him to Bovrik and Lady Mandible. For the last time, Hector hoped.

Bovrik was already at Her Ladyship's chambers, pacing outside the double doors in one of his plainer eyepatches. When he saw Hector he frowned. 'At last,' he said, and took a butterfly box, looked briefly inside, then indicated to Hector to follow.

In her room, Lady Mandible was waiting for them, powdered and painted and coiffured – hair conventional in style but still improbably high – and wearing a surprisingly plain gown. Hector guessed she had not yet dressed for the Feast.

'Your butterflies,' said Bovrik with a flourish, proffering the box. 'It has been a fery successful hatching, if I say so myself.'

Lady Mandible folded down the flaps of the box and almost jumped with delight.

'Oh, they are perfect,' she said, and a wicked smile crossed her face. 'So big, such beautiful colours.' She looked pointedly at Hector. 'What a marvellous job you have done.'

Hector smiled carefully. He would not be drawn in again. But the Baron frowned and stepped closer to Her Ladyship, smiling slightly desperately.

'What *is* that smell?' asked Lysandra.

Bovrik beamed. 'My perfume,' he said. 'The essential oil of the plant *Lippia citriodora*. I have worn extra for tonight.' Heartened by her interest in him he went on, 'Will you not tell me now, Your Ladyship, what you plan to do with the butterflies at the Feast? Haf I mentioned I haf my own surprise, of which I dare to think you will approve . . . ?'

Lysandra was hardly listening. She was too distracted looking at the butterflies in her box and cooing softly.

Chapter Twenty-Nine

The Feasting Begins

All day long carriages had been arriving in convoy up the rocky hill to Withypitts Hall. They carried within them the self-styled elite of Urbs Umida, some rather higher up the social scale than others, but all with plenty of money or land.

Surprisingly – or unsurprisingly perhaps, dissatisfaction being the curse of the well off – emanating from these carriages were numerous complaints about the state of the road, the distance of the journey, the weather and suchlike. And, of course, there were the ever-present expressions of anxieties: that one might be seated at a disadvantage around the table, or that a particular person would or wouldn't be there.

The gates to Withypitts Hall were manned by guards resplendent in full uniform, displaying the Mandible colours, a rather gaudy yellow and bright green. The gold-leaf-edged invitations were presented and, once carefully scrutinized (it was not unknown for forgeries to be made), the guests were waved through.

As they stepped down from their carriages the ladies stole sly glances from behind their fans at the attire of their companions in line, reassuring themselves that they were better dressed. They knew, however, that not one of them could hope to outshine Lady Mandible. Indeed, it would have been unforgivable to even try! As for the men, they were no less vain and had perfected the art of instantly assessing each other's outfit in a single rapid upward sweep of the eyes (one always started with the shoes). *They* had for competition Baron Bovrik de Vandolin.

By the stroke of seven everyone was seated at the huge dining table but there was no sign of the hosts. What matter! The honeyed wine was already flowing freely, and when the half-hour struck tongues were loose, eyes were bright, laughter was high-pitched and table manners were hardly in evidence. There were 'oohs' and 'aahs' as the guests admired the Hall and each other. The table, which was dangerously overladen, groaned with food and an excess of cutlery and silver. An excess because the more that was consumed by glass, the less was consumed by tine and blade, fingers being the preferred choice.

The revellers, each and every one, ate as if there was no tomorrow. What a feast it was! What a fellow this Trimalchio must have been! As fast as a pitcher of wine or a plate of food was brought out, it was emptied and another was demanded. Up and down the length of the table gaping mouths and drooling dribbling chins were the order of the day, and the beleaguered servers were grabbed by one fellow and tugged by another until their tunics were practically torn asunder.

Hector, keeping a low profile, observed it all from the sidelines. How could he resist seeing the denouement of so much preparation before he left the Hall forever? And of course there was the small matter of his butterflies. He watched the guests feed, hand to plate to mouth, hand to plate to mouth, in a ceaseless repetition. Dormouse tails (apparently particularly delicious) dangled from their lips; entire sparrows dropped into their gaping maws; fat plums and cherries ready to burst were forced into their mouths until the juices squirted in all directions. This was not hunger, this was sheer unadulterated gluttony.

Seeking respite from it all, Hector turned away to see Bovrik hovering around the end of the table looking decidedly ill at ease. As was expected, the Baron was eye-catching in his apparel of midnight blue and apricot with hints of violet, but Hector was somewhat surprised to see that he was wearing an eyepatch. On a night such as this he thought he would be showing off one of his garish eyeballs. Watching Bovrik wringing his hands and shooting his cuffs repeatedly made Hector himself anxious, so he chose the lesser of two evils and looked again to the table.

Down in the kitchen, by now a steaming hellish place, Mrs Malherbe and her minions were labouring away. Every minute a servant would rush in and demand more food, more drink, more everything! There was hardly enough room to move what with the piles of food, both dead and alive, stacked up in every available space and the extra people running about. And the noise! Orders, often conflicting, were barked out, pots and pans were slammed down, food slopped over the sides, and the air was blue with the language.

'Nobles, they call themselves,' muttered Mrs Malherbe as she abused the pastry for another pudding. 'They are like animals up there. And what have they provided towards tonight? Nowt! All the ordinary people, the farmers and hunters and shepherds, the real providers of food, where are they, I ask you? Not here, not on your life!'

Back upstairs, as the guests took a breather after what had proved to be only the first course, the doors to the great hall were at last flung open to the sound of a trumpet fanfare. Hector looked up.

'Please be upstanding for His Lordship Lord Burleigh Mandible and his beautiful wife, Lady Lysandra Mandible,' came the cry and all stumbled to their feet, belching and with buttons straining, clutching their glasses and goblets.

Lysandra entered the hall first and there was an immediate muted gasp of surprise. She was radiant, there was no doubt about that, in a cream dress that sparkled with diamonds and glowed with pearls. But it was remarkably understated. This was not what the ladies had anticipated at all and there was a palpable feeling of disappointment. All had been led to believe that her outfit would be unrivalled in its splendour. After all that fuss, could this really be it?

Seemingly unconcerned by the reaction, Lady Mandible acknowledged her guests with a nod and the slightest of

F. E. Higgins

smiles, then took her place at the centre of the table on one of the bespoke thrones that she had ordered solely for this occasion. Now all eyes turned back to the doors in readiness for her husband. And for once he didn't disappoint. In fact, tonight Lord Mandible actually upstaged his wife.

And how did he do that? What was so marvellous about his entrance? Was it that he came into the dining hall on horseback? Certainly that caught the guests' attention. Or maybe it was his attire, for he had chosen to ape a primitive hunter with a huge bearskin over his shoulders and a horned helmet on his head.

In fact, it was neither of these, but that which came in his wake: a Hairy-Backed Forest Hog – the biggest ever – carried aloft on a silver platter by six serving men. At the sight of it Lord Mandible received a standing ovation. It was certainly deserving of this reaction. The hog, its crackling still hissing and spitting from the roasting and shining with honey glaze, sat on a bed of golden ivy leaves. It wore a rather surprised expression on its elongated face, as if even in death it did not expect to be here. On the tip of each lower curved canine there was a large golden apple (Lord Mandible's idea) and on its head a sort of glittering tiara (also Mandible's idea). Arranged

224

along its sides were roasted piglets with live thrushes stuffed in their mouths which kept escaping to the hall ceiling and roosting up there. Several guests looked a bit flummoxed by this, particularly when they had to dodge droppings, but it seemed best not to say anything out loud.

The men carrying the platter placed it carefully on a prepared raised stand at the end of the table where it could be seen by all. Lord Mandible dismounted, in his usual (perhaps better described as 'unusual' on account of his leg) fashion, and joined his wife on his matching throne. There was more cheering and applause and general uproar until he held up his hand for attention. In the past it was well known that Lord Mandible had found the Midwinter Feast a bit of a chore but his Hairy-Back triumph had evidently changed that, and he was about to make a speech.

Hector couldn't help noticing, however, that Lady Mandible was watching everything in uncharacteristic silence. He was immediately suspicious. Where were the butterflies? His frayed nerves could hardly stand the suspense. It was time for her to reveal all.

'My dear guests,' Lord Mandible declared, 'it is my great pleasure to welcome you all to this, the Withypitts Hall

Annual Midwinter Feast. Tonight, however, it is my even greater pleasure to present to you the finest specimen of Hairy-Backed Hog ever seen, felled this day by my own hand.' A great hurrah went up, everyone clashed their goblets and clinked their glasses, and it was some minutes before there was quiet enough for Mandible to continue.

'Now,' he shouted at last, his eyes shining, 'let the Midwinter Feast begin!'

And they set to as if they had suffered months of famine. The hog was carved and before long the room was filled with the sound of flesh being torn apart, teeth gnawing on bone and the chewing of sticky juicy meat. The meat from the middle wasn't even properly cooked, the hog having arrived so late in the day, but the guests were oblivious to this. Other plates kept coming; from strange fish dishes to piles of tarts and honey cakes so high that they threatened to topple and subject all those in the vicinity to a vicious pastry assault. By the time Lord Mandible stood up and rapped on a goblet to get his guests' attention, it was no longer the table that groaned but those who sat at it. His overstuffed audience sat back with shining faces and greasy chins, trying to focus their bloodshot eyes, sucking and picking at their teeth with silver toothpicks. Lady

Lysandra seemed to manage a brief smile that could have been interpreted as gracious, but then again could merely have been a twitch. Hector was sickened to his stomach by it all.

Out of the corner of his eye he saw a couple of servants pull aside a panelled screen at the end of the room to reveal Mandible's harpsichord. But what was that on the floor by the pedals? The servants, too close to notice it at their feet, were busy arranging the music. Hector walked slowly, unobtrusively, over to the instrument. There was something familiar about that shape and colour. 'Oh no!' he muttered with a sinking feeling, for the odd-looking bundle on the floor was none other than Percy, Mandible's remaining cat!

And he was as dead as the Hairy-Backed Hog.

'*Tartri flammis!*' hissed Hector, and quickly he bent and scooped the cat up as Mandible's words came to him on the hot and heavy air.

'Now in Lady Lysandra's honour I am going to play a tune I composed myself for the harpsichord, the very instrument my poor father used to play to me. The words I composed only today, so you will forgive me if the verses are not as polished as they could be.'

Hector froze. He could hardly let Mandible see that his

one remaining cat was dead. There was a time and place for such a revelation. This was neither. In the blink of an eye Hector stuffed the still warm cat down the front of his waistcoat and tightened his belt so it wouldn't fall out. He would have to find an opportunity later to dispose of the animal. He drew back against the drapes as Mandible came limping and rustling over to take his seat. He cut a strange figure in his bearskin cloak and horned hat, now slightly askew, but the guests were past caring. He began to play and sing, sort of:

> I took my musket one winter's morn,
> And filled my pouch with lead.
> 'Where to, my lord?' my servant asked,
> 'To the forest of oak,' I said.

> 'Saddle up my horse, my lad,
> And call my trusty dog.
> I vow today to keep my oath
> And catch me a Hairy-Backed Hog.'

> I rode all day and rode all night,
> And rode all day once more.

And finally when dusk came down
I heard a porcine roar.

From the forest's depths the monster came
Yellow of eye and brown of tusk it
Charged at me with spit and snarls,
So I shot it with my musket.

One shot it took to wound the beast
One more and down it fell,
Its meat for me to roast and eat,
Its soul bound straight for hell!

He finished with a gloriously cacophonous triad and a stiff bow. Hector shook his head in disbelief as the hall resounded with cheers and applause. It was a full four minutes before His Lordship could take his seat again at the table. But then Lady Mandible rose from her seat and silence descended once more.

'I have something to show you too, dear husband. I will return,' she said with an enigmatic smile and left the hall.

Chapter Thirty

— —

A Very Special Gift

In the dining hall, where flames roared in three huge fireplaces and the noise of laughter raised the roof, the Midwinter Feast continued in the absence of Lysandra as yet more dishes were served.

Lord Mandible found his appetite quadrupled by his state of elation following the rapturous reception of his performance on the harpsichord. The applause, the acclaim — it had brought tears to his eyes. He ate hungrily, licking and sucking the grease from his fingers.

My, but it was hot in here tonight! He could feel the sweat running down his forehead. He mopped at his brow again with a sleeve. He felt slightly sick. The hog, what was left of it, stared at him mournfully from the other end of the table but suddenly he couldn't eat another morsel. He took a deep breath. He was sure the feeling would pass. Perhaps the excitement was just a little too much. 'I'm an artist after all,' he said to himself. 'I am highly strung.'

Just then the hall doors began to swing open again. The master of ceremonies rapped twice upon the marble floor with his staff and announced, 'Her Ladyship, Lady Lysandra Mandible.'

Every head turned towards the well-oiled doors as each travelled silently along its slow arc, just skimming the floor. Only when they were fully open did Lady Mandible finally step into view. At first glance she hardly looked any different. She was wearing the same dress as before. She was not holding anything. Lord Mandible was confused.

He sat heavily. He was beginning to wish this was all over. He badly felt the need to lie down. He watched as his wife advanced slowly towards him and noted for the first time, as did the rest of the guests, that she had put on a cloak.

The cloak was made of rich cream velvet and trimmed with snow-white ermine. It sparkled with two silver buttons at her throat and silver thread criss-crossed its expanse of material. But none looked at the buttons, none considered the quality of the ermine, none remarked on the velvet or the way the cloak fell from her shoulders and flowed like water out behind her moving softly over the floor. Instead they wondered aloud, 'What sorcery has a cloak shimmer like that?'

For, as Lady Mandible continued her approach, it truly seemed that the cloak was alive with incandescent colour, and she herself seemed to be surrounded by a misty cloud of sparkling hues. The guests were both bemused and entranced by its beauty. Then, like a wave building as it travelled to shore, the realization of what they beheld slowly dawned on them. Hector, his waistcoat still stuffed with the cat, shook his head in anguished disbelief.

'It cannot be!' they whispered. 'It cannot be!'

For the cloak did move, and it did shimmer, because it really *was* alive, though already in the throes of death. Lysandra held out her arms and slowly turned to fully reveal to her astounded audience the true magnificence of her creation. Her face was a picture of triumph and cruel beauty. Now everyone could see clearly what she had done. Bovrik was rooted to the spot, gazing in open-mouthed wonder at the vision before them.

'Oh no!' whispered Hector in utter horror. Attached to

the fabric, with pins so fine they were invisible, covering almost every inch, from the shoulder to the furthest hem, were huge living butterflies, each flapping uselessly as it slowly released its tenuous grip on life. And the fine colourful mist around Lysandra's head that settled as a glittery powder on her skin was composed of the myriad nacreous scales from their frantic wings.

Chapter Thirty-One

——— ———

Running with Wolves

Hector wrenched his gaze from the awful sight, unable to
bear it, and saw instead Bovrik. He was standing as still as
the numerous statues that decorated the dining hall, utterly
entranced by the butterfly cloak.

Suddenly Lord Mandible pushed back his chair and stood
up. Pale and sweating, trembling visibly, he mopped his face
repeatedly with his wet silk handkerchief as he stumbled
forward. He seemed to be in pain. Two servants tried to
come to his aid but he shook them off. He staggered out
from behind the table, using the carved chair backs for
support. Lady Mandible didn't move; instead she watched
him come to her, her glinting eyes as sharp as blades. Hector,

along with the guests around the hall, was shocked into numbed stillness. Mandible was dragging both feet by now but seemed determined to keep going. His eyes were fixed on his wife. 'Lysandra,' he gasped as at last he reached her side, 'I am not so well. Help me.' Then he clutched wildly at his constricted throat, groaned once and fell to the floor as lifeless as the marble tile upon which his head now lay.

The silence was punctuated by a lone hiccup from one of the tables. Lysandra looked upon the body of her husband and sank, rather dramatically, into the arms of Gerulphus who was standing nearby.

'Call for the castle physician!' ordered the manservant authoritatively. 'Fetch some water!'

The drunken revellers looked on in bleary-eyed confusion and the servants ran hither and thither. Lady Mandible had been taken to her throne where she was being revived with salts by one servant and rapid fanning by another. Someone else was waving a burnt feather under her nose. The cloak lay spread all about her, its terrible beauty stilling as the pinned butterflies were crushed and died.

The physician arrived quickly. He had not far to come, being asleep further down the table (it was he who had hiccuped). He knelt unsteadily beside the motionless body and announced fearfully, 'Lord Mandible is dead.'

Bovrik was the first to react. The faux Baron dashed towards Lady Mandible, pushed aside the servants and with a wild flourish ripped off his eyepatch. So desperate was he to display his new eye that he tilted his head at such an acute angle the diamonds and gold caught the light and instantly his whole head seemed to be surrounded by a glittering, blinding halo. Those nearby actually put up their hands to shield their eyes from the glare. Even Hector, at some distance, had to squint.

'Lysandra,' Bovrik spoke at last, 'do not fear. Your husband may be dead but you will not be alone.' He touched his forefinger to his eye. 'See,' he said. 'My new eye. It is for you, Lysandra; consider it a gift. Impressive, don't you agree? I too can be grand. Am I not worthy of you? Together we could—'

Suddenly Lady Mandible raised a hand and slapped Bovrik hard about the face. Caught off guard he lost his balance and staggered sideways. Something shot past him to land on the floor. And all eyes followed the glittering orb as it rolled across the marble to come to a halt at the dead Lord Mandible's foot: it was Bovrik's golden, bejewelled eyeball.

Spots of colour had come back into Lady Mandible's cheeks and her eyes danced. She stood up. 'Lord Mandible dead?' she roared. 'But how? He was in the best of health only moments ago!' She turned to Bovrik, a look of exaggerated horror on her face. 'And did I hear you correctly? Did you say you wished to step into my dead husband's shoes? Only moments after he passed away? You insolent thieving scoundrel!'

Bovrik dropped to the floor and crawled on his hands and knees to retrieve his precious eye. He dusted it off quickly and pushed it back into the empty socket. He got to his feet. 'No, no,' he tried to protest. 'I merely meant . . .' His voice tailed off. No one was listening to him. All ears were attuned to Lady Mandible. An almost imperceptible smile manifested itself on her lips, and with that smile Bovrik suddenly understood that something truly dreadful was happening.

'I wonder, Baron,' mused Lysandra coldly and clearly for everyone to hear, 'if perhaps *you* had something to do with my husband's death.'

'It could be a case of poisoning,' said the physician helpfully. 'His Lordship's lips are quite blue.'

Poison! Murder! The Baron? The guests gasped as one.

237

But Hector could only shake his head in disbelief. Was that why Bovrik had been sneaking about at night? To plot the murder of Lord Mandible? He could hardly believe he hadn't thought of it before. But, even if he had, would it have made any difference? Would he have done something to stop it? Hector was confused. He couldn't answer these questions. His thoughts were lost in a fog.

Bovrik's face was by now drained of all colour as the full horror of what was happening sank in. 'Lady Mandible,' he was whispering, 'surely you cannot believe . . . surely you wouldn't accuse me . . .'

'It would suit you to have him gone, wouldn't it, Baron?' she hissed back.

Bovrik looked around the hall, at the flushed faces watching his every move, at the servants whose lives he had made hell, at Lady Mandible who had turned against him, and he knew he had no chance. With a cry like a wounded animal he turned and fled.

Slowly, with the aid of Gerulphus, Lysandra walked over to Lord Mandible's body. 'Oh, my dear,' she sighed with a very small sob, 'what shall I do without you?'

Hector took one last look at the guests about him . . . and he saw no true sorrow or regret. His stomach turned and he felt only utter revulsion and self-loathing.

'I have become a wolf,' he whispered, and despair coursed through his veins. He thought he might collapse. Is it really too late? he wondered. A slight glimmer of hope began to surface. Perhaps not, he thought. But before he could do anything, from the corridor beyond the dining hall came the sound of galloping hoofs and deep throaty grunts, breaking glass and crockery and high-pitched screams of terror. Up and down the table the guests turned their gaze from Lysandra and the motionless Mandible to hearken at the discord beyond the doors.

And it was not what they heard that struck fear into their hearts but what they saw: a long-tusked monster of enormous proportions hurtling into the hall and skidding to a halt on the marble floor. For the second time in his life, Hector found himself staring into the narrow yellow eyes of a Hairy-Backed Hog. And, unlike the one on the silver platter, this pig was most definitely alive.

Nobody moved a muscle. The beast advanced slowly, breathing heavily, towards the table, its head turning from side to side until its gaze fell on the ravaged skeleton of the roast hog. It gave a long shrill squeal of unmitigated anguish until the crystal chandeliers above shattered and fell like rain on the paralysed crowd below. And then the hog charged.

As Hector ran from the hall the last thing he saw was Gerulphus throwing himself between Lady Mandible and the stampeding hog.

Chapter Thirty-Two

Revelation

Hector knew he had to reach Bovrik's tower quickly. His father was right, Polly was right, the strange prisoner in the tower was right, but it had taken this dreadful night for Hector to realize it.

And now he might be too late.

By the time he reached Bovrik's room, having ascended the stairs three and four at a time, he could hardly speak. But he could smell Bovrik's perfume persisting in the air outside the door, so he knew he was still there.

'Let me in,' he gasped. 'It's Hector.' He slumped against the door. It opened under his weight and he fell forward into the room.

Bovrik was standing by the window, his garish and obscene eye reflecting the candlelight. It looked odd, somehow, and Hector suddenly realized there was a huge crack across the surface of the glass.

'What do you want?' growled Bovrik. He was pale and the left side of his face was slightly red and swollen. From Lady Mandible's slap, thought Hector.

'The box,' he said urgently, dragging himself up to standing. 'Have you opened it?'

Bovrik glanced to his left and Hector saw the small white box still on the chair where he had left it earlier. Bovrik went immediately to pick it up.

'No,' cried Hector. 'Don't open it!'

'Why not?' asked Bovrik. 'It is mine, a gift from Lysandra.' He held out the card, clearly addressed to Baron Bovrik de Vandolin and signed with a swirling L.

Hector took a step forward. 'It's not from Lysandra. It's from me. And now I want it back.'

'From you?' Bovrik put his ear to the box. 'There's something in here,' he said. 'I can hear it.' He looked expectantly at Hector.

'It's full of butterflies, *Pulvis funestus*, Blackwing, but you mustn't open it. They will kill you.' He held out his hands pleadingly.

'Kill me?' Bovrik narrowed his eyes and laughed sarcastically. 'Are they trained to attack?'

Hector shook his head. 'I sprinkled their wings with the poison of a deadly mushroom. If you touch them, you will die. Your lemon scent will drive them wild and draw them straight to you!'

Bovrik smiled slightly. 'My, my! Fery inventive. And hard to detect after, I imagine.' To Hector's relief, he put the box down on the table. 'But why would you send me such a fatal gift?'

Hector's hands hung down at his sides in despair. He had dreamed of this moment so many times, but this wasn't how it was supposed to be, this wasn't how he was supposed to feel. 'Because,' he said heavily, 'you are Gulliver Truepin and I am Hector Fitzbaudly. You blackmailed my father, and by your actions you *killed* him.'

'Hah!' exclaimed Bovrik. 'You seek revenge?' Now he understood and finally let his accent slip. 'Commendable in one so young. You have a bright future. But then why warn me?'

Why? thought Hector. Because my father believed in me. Because I am not like you. Because I am better than that.

243

'Because I am not a wolf,' he said quietly. Bovrik frowned. 'I changed my mind,' he said louder. 'You're finished here at Withypitts Hall. You murdered Lord Mandible and were caught. The guards are probably on their way already. That's revenge enough for me.'

'That is not true. It's all been a mistake,' said Bovrik to Hector's surprise, massaging his puffy cheek. It was quite red by now and the eye was closing. 'I did not kill Mandible, but you're right to say I am finished at Withypitts Hall. I should never have stayed so long. It was misjudgement on my part. Now out of my way, boy, or you'll go the same way as your father.'

'Wait,' Hector said. 'I saw you, creeping about the corridors at night, in and out of Mandible's rooms. I don't know how you did it, but who else has as good a reason as you to want him dead? You said as much tonight, to Lady Mandible.'

'My, you have been keeping an eye on me!' Bovrik raised his eyebrows. 'But you've got it wrong, butterfly boy. The only time I entered Lord Mandible's chambers was to steal his stupid cat for the cat-eater! The rest of the time you saw me, well, let's just say, helping myself to extraneous treasures, to sell. It's in my nature. We all have to make a living. I'm not saying I didn't wish that fool Mandible out of the picture, but my plans in that respect weren't quite as advanced as yours for me!'

Hector was horrified. Here he was thinking that he was better than Bovrik, whereas in fact he was worse. How could he have let himself sink so low?

'But you said you had a surprise for Lady Mandible,' he stuttered.

'Yes, my new eyeball,' said Bovrik impatiently, and he thrust his face towards Hector so he could see it up close. 'Lysandra appreciates beauty. I just wanted to show her that I did too. We could have achieved so much,' he said dreamily, 'but it's all gone wrong.' He rubbed at his eye again, more vigorously. 'This is not such a good fit after all,' he murmured and flipped open the lid of his eyeball box. There they sat, like six silent witnesses.

'How odd,' he said. 'They are mixed up.' He looked up once more at Hector and started. 'What in the name of Hades is that?'

Hector glanced down at his waistcoat and saw too the furry tail emerging from below it. 'It's Percy,' he remembered. 'I found him dead under the harpsichord.' He pulled out the stiffening creature and at the same time something heavy and glittering fell out of his pocket on to the bearskin rug where it gleamed in the fur. He stooped to pick it up.

'At least Mandible went out on a high note,' continued Bovrik. 'His father couldn't play for toffee either. He died alone at his instrument.'

Hector frowned as he straightened. 'He died at the harpsichord?'

'Yes. Didn't you know? Not long after Lysandra married Mandible.' Bovrik looked at Hector, who was examining closely the small item that had fallen from his pocket. It was the dark-stoned ring that he found when last collecting the hog-bristle. Suddenly his blood ran cold. '*Tartri flammis!*' he breathed. 'It's Lady Mandible's.' He turned to Bovrik, wild-eyed. 'I had it all wrong. Don't you see? It's Lady Mandible. *She's* the only other person with something to gain if Lord Mandible is dead. She killed Mandible's father. And she killed Mandible too. But it is you who are to take the blame.'

Bovrik's face contorted in agonized disbelief. 'No,' he wailed. 'It cannot be possible. I, the greatest trickster of them all, have been outdone.'

Chapter Thirty-Three

View from the Top

As he fell he smiled.

So this was what it was like to fly! He could feel the winter air cooling his burning cheeks and it was surprisingly pleasant. He had the sensation that he might be swooping. His eyes were closed and he felt as if his arms were outstretched. It was true, then, what he had heard. Your life did flash before you. It was all there, in no particular order – a cornucopia of little pictures, each a reminder of a thousand different things.

Now he was in the forest again. The leaves were brown and damp and he could smell the rot. He heard the rooting of a hog and immediately the acrid aroma of singed flesh and hair made his nose sting. That man, the traveller, he was there too but then he was gone, replaced by Hector's inquisitive face.

'Good luck to you,' he thought, opening his fingers wide to allow the wind to rush through.

He turned, slowly he felt, in the air and continued to fall. He wondered why it was taking so long. As he passed down the side of the tower he could see the smallest of things in minute detail, which was strange because it was late evening and only the distant stars and the full moon lit the sky. And he knew in reality he must be falling at speed, yet he was able to look at each thing slowly and take it in: the moss between the bricks, an insect crawling across the rough stone, a green rivulet where the rain followed a crooked path down the wall.

He was confused by a mixture of emotions: sadness, regret, anger, frustration. Had there not been a single moment of happiness? he wondered. And then *she* appeared. She was smiling, holding out her hand as she had done a hundred times or more. He pursed his lips as if to kiss it but she drew back and her eyes became cold.

'What a fool I was,' he thought. 'What a foo—'

He landed and lay crookedly on his side in a spreading pool of dark red blood. And the last thing Bovrik saw was his own reflection in the shining orb that rolled away from him.

Chapter Thirty-Four

Departure

'Quick! Lord Mandible has been murdered, the killer is on the run and Lady Mandible's life is in danger from a rampaging hog! You must go immediately to the great dining room!'

The guard at the top of the tower gaped at Hector for a moment before gathering his weapons and clattering down the tower stairs as fast as he was able.

Working rapidly, Hector unlocked the heavy cell door with the key he had taken from the Baron's room. The prisoner was already waiting on the other side. 'I knew you wouldn't forget me.' He grinned.

'How could I leave you here?' asked Hector. 'I owe you

my life! Besides, I have some questions for you. But later. Let's go.'

Below, the corridors were deserted. As they approached the main doors both Hector and his companion could hear the roars and grunts still emanating from the dining hall. The hog had been locked in and the huntsmen were busy debating how best to capture the beast. News had spread quickly of Bovrik's fall, and those who had escaped the hog uninjured now rushed outside to look at his broken body. As a result the fleeing pair escaped Withypitts without hindrance to head for the stables.

At the edge of the forest Hector pulled up his horse and looked at his companion.

'Who are you?' he asked at last. 'And why have you been following me?'

'My name,' the young man replied, 'is Ludlow Fitch.'

Hector's mouth fell open. 'Lottie Fitch's son?'

Ludlow nodded. 'And Polly's friend. She was very concerned for your safety so I promised to follow you, to help you if I could. But I cannot deny I had my own reason for doing so. You know little of my business, Hector, but I thought perhaps you could become my apprentice.'

Hector shook his head ashamedly. 'You don't want me,' he mumbled. 'Or at least you wouldn't if you knew what terrible thing I came close to doing.' He wheeled his horse about to see again the ominous silhouette of Withypitts Hall. 'I can hardly bear to think on it. In that place . . . I was not myself.' And he swallowed a huge sob and hunched further into his horse's saddle.

Ludlow put a hand on his arm. 'A friend of mine used to say, "You cannot change the past, but every moment is an opportunity to change your future."'

Hector wiped his nose on his sleeve. 'He sounds like a good friend.'

'He was like a father to me.'

'I had a father. What I did, I did for him. But he would not be proud of me, of what I nearly became.'

'One day you will tell me what you did,' said Ludlow softly. 'And I'll guard your secret. But for now we should keep moving.'

Hector felt his temple gingerly. His musket wound was stinging in the cold air. 'I was to go back to the City,' he said.

'Come with me,' urged Ludlow. 'I know a place in the mountains where we can be safe, the Atrium Arcanorum.'

'A Hall of Secrets,' said Hector in surprise.

'Yes.' Ludlow nodded. 'A wondrous place. You have never seen its like. I have a friend there: Juno. She can heal your wound; she is a marvel with herbs. But perhaps you wish to part company. After all, your debt is paid.'

Hector shook his head. 'Not quite. What about the Landlord's Pickle?'

Ludlow laughed. 'Tell me on the way,' he said, and trotted off.

Hector took one last look at Withypitts Hall then spurred his horse forward. 'What sort of apprentice?' he called to Ludlow. Ludlow looked back over his shoulder.

'That's a whole other story,' he said.

Chapter Thirty-Five

A Letter to Polly

Hall of Secrets

Dear Polly,

    I have one more story to tell, perhaps the worst
of all. We already know the fate of Posset, eaten by
a Frenchman, but what of her companion? Poor Percy, he
died simply because he walked across the harpsichord
keys. Lady Mandible poisoned them (or maybe Gerulphus
did it for her) with the same mushroom poison I
collected in the forest. Little did Perigoe know how
useful 'Myths and Folklore, Flora and Fauna of the
Ancient Oak Forest' would be!

    Lady Mandible knew that her husband was to play

at the Feast. What a perfect setting for her fatal drama. He absorbed the poison through his fingers and then through his mouth when he was stuffing himself at the Feast. I suspect that is how she killed Mandible's father too. And what of her previous husbands? The thought is almost too much to bear! As for her reason: money and power, I reckon. But also, terrible though it is to contemplate, maybe even for her own pleasure.

I told Bovrik as soon as I realized. Having warned him of the toxic butterflies, suddenly I wanted to do everything in my power to save him. I suppose, having come to my senses, I wanted to make up for the fact that I had planned such a dreadful revenge.

In the moments after I told him Bovrik seemed very thoughtful, gazing back down at his precious eyeballs. Then he picked up the box of butterflies.

I held out my hand, thinking he was going to give it to me, but before I could stop him, with a cry of anguish, he ripped it open. Instantly a thick cloud of black-winged butterflies flew forth and swarmed around his head, creating a shadowy, dusty, fluttering fog.

'What are you doing?' I screeched. But it was too late. I didn't dare go near him for fear of the poison.

Bovrik slapped wildly at the agitated butterflies, crushing them against his face and neck until his hands were dripping with glutinous guts and then, when I thought it could get no worse, he smeared the toxic slime across his mouth.

'Tartri flammis!' I cried, and stepped back. 'You are a lunatic.'

Bovrik turned to me, his face a grotesque mask of insect innards. 'How long will it take,' he said, 'before I die?'

'A short while,' I whispered, 'and it will be painful.'

'She has done me in anyway,' he said cryptically. 'I thought this might be quicker.' There was a strange look in his eyes, almost of triumph. 'No man, or woman, decides my fate,' he said firmly. Then, before I could stop him, he ran across the room and jumped through the window.

I realize now I have not been myself for some time, even before I came to Withypitts Hall. My father, you and Ludlow were right all along. Revenge is not the answer. If I had followed its soul-destroying path to the end, I would have been nothing less than a cold-blooded murderer. That was not what my father had in mind for me. By pretending I was someone I was not,

The Eyeball Collector

I was no better than Truepin (whatever his real identity was. I wonder if he even knew any more). So blinded was I by my all-consuming anger that I failed to see it was not the Baron I should fear; the riddle was not what he was up to, but what evil plans were being laid by Lady Mandible.

But that is enough of this story. I think finally I can lay down my quill. I am in a different place now, with new friends, and the future, though uncertain, looks bright. And soon, dear Polly, I will be on my way back to you.

Salve,
Your friend,
Hector

Chapter Thirty-Six

❧   ❧

Article from

The Northside Diurnal Journal

A quality daily newspaper for the discerning reader

Strange Happenings at Withypitts Hall
By
Tarquin Faulkner

The Midwinter Feast has proved to be an unfortunate and rather gruesome occasion for Withypitts Hall this year. A week on and still it is the talk of the town. Not only did Lord Mandible collapse and die at the harpsichord (after an apparently brilliant performance on said instrument), but Baron Bovrik de Vandolin was also found dead at the foot of his tower. It is believed he took his own life to evade trial, having been accused of the murder of Lord Mandible.

And that is not the end of it. The very same evening a Hairy-Back she-hog went on the rampage at the Hall, killing many revellers and wounding others. Most likely she was seeking revenge for the death (and consumption) of her mate. Witnesses report that Lady Mandible was one of the first to die at the pig's tusks, but to date her body has not been recovered. Others claim that her personal manservant threw himself heroically between her and the hog and saved her life. Whatever the case, neither one has been seen since. Rumour has it that somehow the two of them escaped and have fled the country. A reliable source of mine, recently returned from abroad, swears blind he saw her at the court of a European prince, but unfortunately he has no proof.

And one last puzzle remains: the six dead servants found in various parts of Withypitts in the early hours after the ill-fated Feast. There is no evidence that the hog killed them, but each held in his hand one of the Baron's famous bejewelled eyes, purloined, no doubt, after his death . . .

A Note from F. E. Higgins

I too was puzzled by the dead servants and I wished that I had Hector at hand to help solve the riddle! In his absence I went back through all my papers and documents and eventually I pieced together what I think happened.

Hector admitted to spreading the wings of the black butterflies with poison from the forest mushroom *Stipitis longi*. This is what he was crushing in his pestle and mortar and why he was wearing gloves.

Stipitis longi is closely related to the Amanita family of mushrooms, containing some of the deadliest fungi in the world. When Lysandra's ring was dislodged from Hector's pocket (the ring he picked up in the forest), he realized that she too must have been collecting the mushrooms.

She spread the poison on the harpsichord keys to kill Mandible. Percy was just in the wrong place at the wrong time. But what Hector didn't know was that she had also smeared it on Bovrik's golden eye, the eye he made such a fuss about wearing at the Feast. In fact she left nothing to chance, and tainted all of his eyeballs. That is why they were out of order in the box. Hence the death of the servants too. What a high price all paid for pilfering! But, as we know, Lady Mandible lived by her own rules. And by killing the Baron she also ensured he could not defend himself against her accusations of murder.

When Hector told the Baron his suspicions about the harpsichord, Bovrik realized immediately who had disturbed his eyeballs. And of course his new eye, the seventh, was already irritating him. Knowing he was going to die anyway, Bovrik chose to release the poisoned butterflies, hoping to speed up the process. I imagine he thought eating the poison would move things along more quickly than the gradual absorption his tainted eye promised. I cannot help but think, though, that to be tricked by Lady Mandible must have been too much to bear for the swindler Truepin. Ultimately, faced with such a painful death, he wished to be the master of his own destiny and he jumped.

I have the seventh eye, Bovrik's gold-rimmed and diamond-studded masterpiece. It is cracked and time-worn, and thankfully no longer toxic, though I always wear gloves when I handle it. And of all the objects I have acquired on my own journey, from Pagus Parvus to Urbs Umida and beyond, I think it is the one that fascinates me the most.

Finally, those of you who have been with me since the beginning of my adventures will know that even now not all mysteries have been solved. I cannot promise that they ever will be, but I am closer now than ever, as you might understand when you learn under what hallowed roof I write.

F. E. Higgins
Atrium Arcanorum

Postscript

If you would know more about Hector and Ludlow's world, read first *The Black Book of Secrets*, where in many ways the story began, and then *The Bone Magician*. *The Bone Magician* is what I like to call a 'paraquel' — neither sequel nor prequel, but a story in parallel. In the same vein, I like to think of *The Eyeball Collector* as a 'polyquel', for it contains elements from both stories as well as mysteries all of its own.

Appendix I

Riddle Solutions

The Kingdom Where It Was a Crime to Tell a Lie
(Page 8) The man answers, 'I will be burned'. This threw the king into such confusion that he had to release him.

'E'
(Page 27) The answer, 'senselessness', is arrived at by breaking up the word into three parts – sense/less/ness i.e. the word 'sense' *less* the letters 'n e s s'. This leaves a single 'e'.

The Landlord's Pickle
(Page 62. See if you can make it work!)

Ten weary footsore travellers,
All in a woeful plight,
Sought shelter at a wayside inn
One dark and stormy night.

'Nine rooms, no more,' the landlord said
'Have I to offer you,
To each of eight a single bed,
But the ninth must serve for two.

A din arose. The troubled host
Could only scratch his head,
For of those tired men no two
Would occupy one bed.

The puzzled host was soon at ease –
He was a clever man –
And so to please his guests devised
This most ingenious plan.

In a room marked A two men were placed,
The third was lodged in B,
The fourth to C was then assigned,
The fifth retired to D.

In E the sixth he tucked away
In F the seventh man,

The eight and ninth in G and H,
And then to A he ran,

Wherein the host, as I have said,
Had laid two travellers by;
Then taking one – the tenth and last –
He lodged him safe in I.

Nine single rooms – a room for each –
Were made to serve for ten;
And this it is that puzzles me
And many wiser men.

The Evil Queen and the Two Black Stones

(Page 130) Knowing there were two black stones in the bag the young lad reached in and took one out but quickly dropped it before it could be seen and it was lost in the gravel.

'Never mind. Let us see what is left in the bag,' said the young lad. 'If it is a white stone then we know that mine was black, but if it is a black stone then we know that mine must have been white.'

Of course it was black and the lady had to honour her promise and allow him home.

The Land of Liars and Truthtellers

(Page 186) He said to one man, 'If I asked your friend which fork to take, what would he say?' He listened to the answer and then he took the opposite fork.

Think about it . . . it works.

Appendix II

Tartri flammis!
One of Hector's favourite sayings; roughly translated it
means 'By the flames of hell'.

Appendix III

Lepidoptery

Lepidoptery is more commonly known as the collecting, studying or observing of butterflies and moths. The discipline, although popular from as early as the seventeenth century, rose to prominence during the 1900s, when the quest for knowledge and understanding of the natural world entered a stage of swift progression.

The process of lepidoptery starts with the capture of a live specimen in the wild or by a collector breeding a species themselves, as Hector did for Lady Mandible in his purpose-built *Incunabulorum*. Butterflies are captured in large nets or in specially designed traps before being carefully placed into a killing jar, which is filled with poisonous gas for a quick and effective death.

Once the insect's body has thoroughly dried out and rigor mortis has taken its firm hold, the lepidopterist must soften the joints of the delicate creature to restore the exothermic frame (the hard outer body of the insect) and wings to their former glory. Holding the specimen gently between thumb and forefinger, the lepidopterist injects boiling water into the rear of the thorax (the part between the neck and the abdomen), using a very fine-needled syringe, until the water starts to dribble out and the insides become malleable.

Then the butterfly is placed into a container lined with damp cloth, known as a relaxing box. A fine mist of water is sprayed over the wings to aid the process before the lid is sealed and it is left for an hour. On returning to the relaxing box, the collector grips the base of the butterfly's wings tightly and moves them up and down, as if the creature were flying. Gradually the muscles loosen and then finally give way completely. The now subservient butterfly is ready for positioning.

The lepidopterist grasps the specimen firmly and pushes a large pin directly through the centre of the thorax, ensuring it is perfectly vertical, then continues to ease the pin through the entire body until it emerges on the other side, through the middle of the legs. Now the butterfly is pinned very precisely on to a display board, with the colourful wings spread and fixed using smaller pins – inserted between the two veins on the forewings – to hold the insect for eternity in its magnificent shape.

Finally the specimen must be labelled, detailing its breed and the time and place of capture, or place of breeding. The board is mounted inside a glass-covered box and displayed, enabling the collector to admire his or her butterfly for evermore.

A selected list of titles available from Macmillan Children's Books

The prices shown below are correct at the time of going to press. However, Macmillan Publishers reserves the right to show new retail prices on covers, which may differ from those previously advertised.

F. E. Higgins

The Black Book of Secrets	978-0-330-44405-7	£5.99
The Bone Magician	978-0-330-44482-8	£5.99

Carole Wilkinson

Dragonkeeper: Dragon Dawn	978-0-230-74365-6	£8.99
Dragonkeeper	978-0-330-44109-4	£5.99
Dragonkeeper: Garden of the Purple Dragon	978-0-330-44112-4	£5.99
Dragonkeeper: Dragon Moon	978-0-330-47207-4	£5.99

Elizabeth Laird

Secrets of the Fearless	978-0-330-43466-9	£5.99
Lost Riders	978-0-330-45209-0	£5.99

All Pan Macmillan titles can be ordered from our website, www.panmacmillan.com, or from your local bookshop and are also available by post from:

Bookpost, PO Box 29, Douglas, Isle of Man IM99 1BQ

Credit cards accepted. For details:
Telephone: 01624 677237
Fax: 01624 670923
Email: bookshop@enterprise.net
www.bookpost.co.uk

Free postage and packing in the United Kingdom